RONI'S SWEET FIFTEEN

"We need another rehearsal," Greg said. "Those scenery changes just aren't working yet and the lighting is terrible. We'll have to have a technical run-through tomorrow night."

"But that's Friday, Greg. I have a date," someone yelled.

"And I have a big party," I said.

"I'm sorry, guys," Greg said. "I did tell you to keep the final weekend free, so no excuses. I want everybody here at six. If you work well, we'll be out of here by ten."

Ten o'clock, on the night of my family party? Somehow I didn't think they'd understand. I went up to Greg. "Do you really, really need me?" I asked. "All my relatives have come into town for my party. My mother is goig to be so mad . . ."

"Sorry, Roni," he said. "You're too important. You'll have to tell your folks that you have to be here."

Janet Quin-Harkin was born in Bath and educated in England, Austria and Germany. She studied dance and drama as a child and went straight from college to work for the BBC, where she wrote several plays.

Yearning for sunshine she went to Australia to work for Australian Broadcasting. Within weeks she was given a contract to draw a daily cartoon for the *Australian* newspaper. In Sydney she met her husband. The Quin-Harkins moved to California, where they lived for twenty years and raised four children.

Janet Quin-Harkin began writing children's books when living in San Francisco. Her first picture book, *Peter Penny's Dance*, won many awards, including *The New York Times* Best Book of the Year Award. She has subsequently written more than fifty books for young adults.

Janet Quin-Harkin is now a full-time writer and also teaches creative writing at a nearby college.

Roni's
sweet fifteen

Also available in the Boyfriend Club series

the boyfriend club

9

Roni's sweet fifteen

JANET QUIN-HARKIN

PUFFIN BOOKS

PUFFIN BOOKS

Published by the Penguin Group
Penguin Books Ltd, 27 Wrights Lane, London W8 5TZ, England
Penguin Books USA Inc., 375 Hudson Street, New York, New York 10014, USA
Penguin Books Australia Ltd, Ringwood, Victoria, Australia
Penguin Books Canada Ltd, 10 Alcorn Avenue, Toronto, Ontario, Canada M4V 3B2
Penguin Books (NZ) Ltd, 182–190 Wairau Road, Auckland 10, New Zealand

Penguin Books Ltd, Registered Offices: Harmondsworth, Middlesex, England

First published in the USA by Troll Associates Inc. 1995
Published in Puffin Books 1995
1 3 5 7 9 10 8 6 4 2

Produced by Daniel Weiss Associates Inc.
33 West 17th Street, New York, NY 10011, USA

The moral right of the author has been asserted

Made and printed in England by Clays Ltd, St Ives plc

For my brother who has become friend as well as relative, and for Jan, a great sister-in-law.

1

I was on my way to meet my friends for lunch when it happened: I was kidnapped by nerds. When I was little, I used to have this nightmare in which horrible monsters leaped out at me and grabbed me with slimy hands. They wouldn't let go even though I struggled and screamed. I never dreamed it would actually happen.

I bet you have at least one nerd in your class— some guy who dresses strangely or carries a briefcase or laughs like a hyena? In the freshman class at Alta Mesa High, we had a whole nerd pack. They did everything together. And their favorite activity seemed to be making life complicated for my friends Ginger, Karen, and Justine, and me. We all found the nerds disgusting, but the nerds seemed to find *us* absolutely fascinating. The more we ran from them, the more they were convinced, with their own weird logic, that we were their soul mates. We'd told them to get lost in every creative way possible, but they kept coming back for more.

Even so, they had never actually tried to kidnap one of us before.

I was late coming out of English class because I'd been fighting for a better grade on my last essay. Mrs. Epstein had given me a C-plus, but I felt that I deserved way better. I know I'm not too hot on English grammar, but the content of my essay was good. Unfortunately, Mrs. Epstein is *very* hot on English grammar. She took off one grade point for each grammatical error. I was tempted to point out to her that it wasn't my fault that Spanish was my first language. I'd like to see her write a whole essay in Spanish! I mean, did grammar really matter, as long as the reader could understand what I was trying to say? Well, it mattered to Mrs. Epstein—and she was the one doing the grading.

Luckily I'm a born fighter. If I think something is unfair, I don't give up until I prove it. I made Mrs. Epstein admit that the content of my essay deserved an A. Then I asked her if a publisher would have turned down an Ernest Hemingway book if he'd made some grammatical errors. Then I reminded her that Shakespeare never spelled words the same way twice. Finally she smiled.

"Okay, Roni, you've convinced me," she said. "You certainly put up a good argument. You should join our debate team."

"You're going to give me an A?" I asked hopefully.

"Don't push your luck," she said, grinning. "Grammar might not have been important to Hemingway's publishers, but it is to me. I'll give you a B and that's my final offer."

I took it. At least it was better than a C-plus. And I was flattered by what she'd said about the debate team. My father always said I could argue the hind leg off a donkey. Maybe it would come in useful one day.

So it was already fifteen minutes into lunch hour as I ran down the empty hallways and out into the hot sunshine. It was almost April, and Phoenix was already beginning to heat up. Soon we'd probably have to abandon our favorite tree and eat lunch in the air-conditioned cafeteria with the three thousand other kids who went to our school.

I didn't sense any danger as I pushed open the

door and stood blinking in the bright light. But suddenly there were hands on me—clammy little hands that pinched.

"Got her!" cried a squeaky voice. "Don't let her get away."

I recognized the squeak instantly. It was Owen—head nerd, leader of the nerd pack, most repulsive of all (although that was a close contest). He was everything you would expect—pint sized, skinny, bony, spike haired, and fond of laughing in a whooping, hideous way. And those are just some of his better features. Now he'd added kidnapping to his list of crimes against good taste.

"What are you doing?" I yelled. "Are you out of your tiny skull? Let go of me!"

"No way," Owen said with a repulsive leer. "We are on a sacred mission. Right, guys?"

"Right," Wolfgang said. He was the super-size nerd, a huge saggy blimp with a face like a deflating balloon, an IQ smaller than his shoe size, and clothes that drive Justine crazy. She's very fashion-conscious, and Wolfgang is definitely the most uncoordinated person I've ever seen. Today he was wearing his famous brown-and-purple stag sweater (even though the temperature was over eighty) with a pair of red baggy pants.

"We were sent to find you and we did," added Ronald the beanpole.

"What are you talking about?" I yelled. "Let go of me! People are looking!" Being seen in the company of nerds would definitely not help my image around school.

"Tell me where you're taking me!" I insisted as they propelled me across the yard. I looked around hopefully for a normal person to rescue me, but the school yard was practically deserted because of the heat. I was alone among nerds.

Walter fell into step beside us as they dragged me protesting across the school yard. He didn't say anything. He hardly ever does. He's the weak, silent type. He nodded solemnly at me.

The only nerd that was missing from the pack on this occasion was Chris. I don't know what to tell you about him, except that he's my boyfriend.

Let me qualify that a little. Chris isn't really a nerd. It's just that he came to Alta Mesa after the school year had started and his locker was right next to Owen's. So Owen was the first person who was nice to him, and he feels grateful. Besides, Chris enjoys the sort of virtual reality stuff that the nerds love. (I think that's because they don't have a *real* reality.) But I have to admit, he does have some nerdy characteristics.

Chris likes watching the science documentaries on public TV—you know, the ones about grotesque insects and crawly things? And he does wear polyester, although I've managed to upgrade his dress habits. He doesn't wear plaid pants anymore, and I helped him pick out a black leather jacket. We're making progress.

You might be asking yourself why a fun, attractive, outgoing girl like me would ever want to date a nerd. It's a good question—I've asked it myself many times. The fact is that Chris has many un-nerdy qualities that make him fun to be with. He does great impressions, and he's very funny. He always keeps me laughing. Also, we're not actually dating. We hang out together, go to movies, and eat pizza, but we aren't officially boyfriend and girlfriend.

Anyway, we hadn't been seeing much of each other recently. I'd been busy with track. I was the star distance runner on the freshman team, which surprised even me. I'd never gone out for school sports before, but I spend a lot of time running, since I'm usually at least ten minutes late everywhere I go. So I guess it came naturally. I'd also been spending time with my best friends. Karen had just broken up with her boyfriend, James, and we'd tried to come up with creative ways to help her get over him. We hadn't expected her to end up with the biggest hunk in the school, but that's another story.

Right now I was about to be dragged into the hallway that contained the locker of every nerd in the school. Don't ask me how the school authorities knew who was a nerd and who wasn't. They just knew. You only had to go into that hall and see the sci-fi posters to know that you had stumbled into a place where no normal person boldly goes.

"Wait a minute," I yelled. "I'm not going in there."

"It's okay. He's waiting for us just inside," Owen assured me, as if I knew what he was talking about. They flew me up the steps, through the doors, and deposited me in front of a very surprised Chris.

"Uh . . . hi, Roni," he stammered. "What are you doing here?"

"Good question," I snapped. "I was dragged here, against my will, by four subhumans."

"We found her, like you said," Ronald said happily.

"*You* organized this?" I demanded angrily. "Did you send your creepy friends to kidnap me?

Wouldn't a simple 'Chris would like to talk to you' be enough? Or you could even have come to find me yourself, if that isn't too much trouble."

He still looked surprised. "That's exactly what I was about to do," he said. "Do you really think I'd send people to get you? You know me better than that."

I had to admit that this was true. Chris had always been the most considerate person around. It was one of the things I liked about him.

"But you said you had to find her right away," Wolfgang growled in his big, deep voice. "So we wanted to help. We found her for you."

Chris gave me an embarrassed smile. "I'm sorry," he said. "Sometimes my friends are a little too enthusiastic."

"Your friends are a little too weird," I said, glaring at the nerds so fiercely that they all took a step backward.

We'd had fights about his continued friendship with the nerds before. I tried to understand why he hadn't told them to jump off the nearest cliff, but quite frankly, I still couldn't figure it out.

"We were only trying to get you two lovebirds together as speedily as possible," Owen said.

"Oh, please," I began, but Chris took my arm.

16

"Let's get out of here," he whispered. "See you later, guys."

With an eager chorus of good-byes sounding behind us, we stepped outdoors to sunlight and sanity.

"How can you stand it?" I demanded. "Why haven't you asked for a new locker yet?"

Chris grinned. "They mean well, Roni. I feel sorry for them. I know what it's like to be teased and made fun of. I was pretty much the class clown at my old school."

"What's this about, anyway?" I asked. "Why did you need to find me in such a hurry?"

"The play," he said, beaming at me excitedly. "Remember last fall when we were in the talent show—"

"When we *won* the talent show," I corrected.

"When we *won* the talent show," he agreed. "That senior guy came up to us and said he wanted to use us in the spring play?"

"I remember."

"Well, I just passed the drama board and they were posting a flyer about the play! They're holding auditions after school tomorrow and Wednesday. We can go see what he has planned for us . . . if you still want to do it."

He looked at me doubtfully.

"Of course I'd like to do it," I said. "It will be fun being in a real play, especially if he gives us the funny parts he promised. Did the flyer say what play it was?"

"*Oklahoma!*"

"*Oklahoma!* That's a musical. I thought it was going to be an ordinary play."

"So?"

"You have to sing and dance to be in a musical. I've never sung or danced in public in my life."

"Me neither, but there's always a first time. And that guy did say that he wanted to use us."

"Yeah, but I got the feeling he had a very different kind of play in mind. A big school musical . . . I can't see two little freshmen getting anything more than chorus parts."

"I don't know about that, Roni," Chris argued. "That guy—Greg something, right?—he was there when I went by, and he asked me to come, and bring you."

"Wow," I said. "Let's do it. What have we got to lose?"

Chris beamed. "I've been waiting for this all year. I was so happy right after the talent show, but then I went back to being just the old, blah me. I guess I want to feel that way again—I've got the theater in my blood now. Do you feel the same?"

"Uh . . . not exactly," I said. He had definitely been around nerds too long. Normal people didn't go around saying things like that. "But it might be fun to be in the musical, even if we only get chorus parts. There's just one small problem . . ."

"What?"

"We have to learn to sing and dance by tomorrow."

Chapter

2

Lunch hour was almost over by the time I finally made it to our tree. I call it that because we'd adopted it as our own personal lunch spot on the first day of school, when we were four new kids who didn't want to face the zillions of strangers in the noisy cafeteria. We couldn't find a place to sit, actually. Nobody would move over for us. That had been the final straw that had driven us outside.

A lot had happened since then. We'd made lots of friends, done all kinds of cool stuff, and found—and lost—boyfriends, but we'd stayed best friends. Ginger and I had known each other since kindergarten, of course, but Karen had come from a Catholic girls' school and Justine from snobby Sagebrush

Academy. I couldn't imagine life without them.

All three looked up with worried faces as I came toward them that afternoon.

"What happened to you?" Ginger called. "We almost ate your brownie, but Karen wouldn't let us."

"Were you with Mrs. Epstein all this time?" Justine asked. "No grade is worth missing food for."

I flopped onto the ground beside them and grabbed the one brownie left on the foil wrapper. "I've been through an ordeal far worse than a fight with a teacher," I said, cramming a large piece into my mouth. "I was kidnapped by nerds."

"You're kidding," Karen said. "They might be gross, but they'd never . . ."

"Believe it," I said. "You could be next."

"Yuck!" Justine made a face. "You mean they really put their slimy little hands on you? Did they take you to their lair? Do they really live in underground caves? Did they try to suck out your brains?"

"This is serious." Ginger giggled. "I always thought the nerds were harmless. Weird, but harmless."

"They are," I said. "It's not as bad as it sounds. They were trying to be helpful in their own bizarre way. Chris told them he had to find me right away, so they found me and dragged me to him."

21

"Boy, does he have nerve," Justine began, but I shook my head.

"He didn't tell them to—he was as embarrassed as I was. He just wanted to find me because he saw a notice about tryouts for the play."

"Tryouts? When?" Ginger asked.

"Tomorrow and Wednesday."

"The director promised you a good part, didn't he?"

"I'm not sure about that," I said. I had finished the brownie and was now chowing down on a huge barbecued beef sandwich. I'm a growing girl, you know. I have what my mother calls a "hearty appetite."

"But he did offer you a part that night after the talent show. We were there—we heard," Ginger insisted.

"I think he might have had another play in mind," I explained. "Something smaller, maybe. They're doing *Oklahoma!* I can't see myself getting a good part in that."

"Why not? The director was impressed with your skit at the talent show," Karen said.

"But a musical is different. I bet everyone has to sing and dance."

"You're absolutely right, Roni," Justine said,

22

stretching out her long legs. "There is no way anyone would give you a part that requires dancing. I've seen you on the dance floor, and frankly, you haven't a clue."

"Thanks for the vote of confidence," I said.

"I didn't mean that in a bad way," Justine said hastily. "All I meant was that you clearly haven't had formal training. It's not your fault you grew up in the boonies where culture doesn't exist. If you'd gone to Sagebrush Academy and taken ballet classes, you'd know how to move with grace, like me. Come to think of it, that's not such a bad idea."

"You're volunteering to coach Roni?" Karen asked.

Justine looked surprised. "Well, I guess I could give her a few pointers. . . . But I was thinking more of myself."

"That's nothing new!" Ginger whispered to me.

Justine stuck out her tongue at Ginger. "I mean I might go to those tryouts myself. After all, tennis is almost over and I need something to keep me amused. With my dancing ability I'm sure to get a good part. Maybe even one of the leads."

"Don't get carried away, Justine," Ginger teased her. "Remember what happened at cheerleading tryouts?"

Justine had insisted that she was an experienced cheerleader and had embarrassed us all by making the pyramid collapse at tryouts.

Justine tossed back her ponytail. "Don't worry, I won't be obnoxious. I'll go to tryouts and if they recognize my incredible ability, then that's not my fault, is it?"

"Did you mean what you said about giving me some pointers?" I asked. "I could really use some help, Justine. You're right, I don't have a clue about dancing."

"But the auditions are tomorrow," Justine said. "I can't cram eight years of ballet into one session."

"I don't need eight years of ballet. Just a few simple moves, a few technical terms, so I don't look like a complete klutz."

"I guess I could do that after school today," Justine said. "We can go to my house. My stepmother had a craving for strawberry cheesecake yesterday, but by the time my father went out and bought one, she'd decided that what she really wanted was mustard pickles."

Justine's stepmother is about to have a baby. I guess women really do get weird cravings at times like that, although I don't remember my mother ever acting funny.

"So there's a whole huge cheesecake in the fridge," Justine finished.

"We'll come too. To give Roni encouragement," Ginger said quickly.

"Yeah! I can play my violin for her to dance to," Karen agreed.

Justine laughed. "Of course you guys can come. Roni and I can't finish a whole cheesecake alone."

"Speak for yourself, Justine," I said.

"It's not fair," Ginger complained. "How can you eat like that and never get fat?"

"It's all the chores I have to do at home," I said. "And I have a feeling it's going to get worse. My birthday is coming up."

"And they make you do extra work as a present?" Karen quipped.

"No, but that's what it will turn out to be," I said. "It's my fifteenth birthday."

"So?" Justine said. "When I turned fifteen, we went to a nice restaurant. Tell your folks to do that."

"You don't happen to be Mexican American," I grumbled. "In our culture we make a big thing of fifteen. It's called our *quinceaños,* and it's like a bar mitzvah and confirmation all rolled into one. Girls get dressed up and presented to the community. In

25

the old days it meant we were being shown off to let everyone know we were old enough to be married."

"That's a great idea! Let's get Roni married off," Karen said, grinning. "The Boyfriend Club can arrange a marriage for you."

"Shut up, you guys," I said, starting to giggle.

"Well, we've gotten the hang of picking the right boyfriends," Ginger said, "so it's the next logical step. I'm sure we can find the right guy for you, Roni."

"But not Chris," Justine said quickly. "We'll find her someone better."

"Drew would have been good," Ginger said, giving me a knowing look. "I can see her married to Drew, can't you?"

She was talking about Drew Howard, the cutest sophomore in school. I had actually dated him for a while, but we'd broken up, as I always knew we would. A girl like me can't keep a guy like Drew. Not that I really minded. I couldn't keep up with his lifestyle anyway. But it *had* been the high point of my life so far. I knew that there would always be a special place in my heart for Drew.

Karen sighed. "He'd make a totally cute bridegroom in his tux."

"Thank you very much for your kind offers of help," I said, "but when I decide to get married, I'll choose my own guy. And that definitely won't be until I've done all the living I want to do."

I broke into a Broadway-style song: "Because I gotta lotta living to do!" I added a dance, for good measure.

Justine shuddered. "That's enough, Roni. But you've convinced me—you really do need help. Dance like that at the tryouts tomorrow and you don't have a prayer."

"Maybe there are some nondancing parts," I said, feeling suddenly like a deflated balloon.

"I've seen *Oklahoma!* a million times," Justine said. "Even the old aunt has to dance."

"Don't worry, Roni," Karen said kindly. "You're a fast learner. I bet Justine can teach you enough to get you through auditions. After that, they'll go for your explosive personality."

"Thanks," I said. "You can be my agent."

"Great. I take fifty percent," Karen said, laughing as I pulled her to her feet.

We headed for the nearest building as the bell sounded. I hadn't finished my lunch, so I tried to cram the last of my banana into my mouth as I threw away my lunch bag. A sudden thought struck me.

"One more thing, Justine. I can bring Chris with me, can't I?"

"A nerd? You want to bring a nerd to my house?" Justine said with exaggerated horror.

"He's not a nerd, Justine."

"Does he still wear polyester pants?"

"Well, sometimes."

"And didn't he tell us about that show he watched on kangaroos being born?"

"I guess . . ."

"Then he's a nerd. Once a nerd, always a nerd. That's what I say."

"But he's also my friend, Justine, and he really does want to get a part in this play. If you want to help de-nerdify him, then let him come. Just think what a part in the school play will do for his image. He might just turn into the hottest guy around, and then you'll wish you'd been nicer to him."

"Yeah, right! And pigs might fly," Justine said, laughing. "Okay, I guess he can come. But I'm warning you, Roni. If a single nerdy friend shows up at my house, you die."

"Don't worry," I said. "No nerdy friends, I promise."

Chris was really excited when I told him I'd arranged a dance lesson for us that afternoon.

"You don't know how much I was worrying about the dancing part," he muttered to me. "I'm sure they don't expect guys to be great dancers, but I know that I'm hopeless. Tell me the truth, Roni—you've seen me dance. I'm pathetic, right?"

"Uh . . . right," I agreed. I didn't bother to elaborate.

"And I really want a part in this play," he said. "I've been thinking about it all year. If Justine can work a miracle, I'll be her slave forever."

"Don't tell Justine that," I said, grinning. "She'll have you following her around the mall, carrying her packages . . . and you hate malls."

"If I get a good part, I'll even do that for her," he said. He grabbed my hands. "Imagine, Roni, you and me on the stage again. Maybe we'll even get the leads!"

"Be real, Chris," I said. "I'd settle for a small, amusing cameo, preferably with no dancing."

"Me too," he said, "but who knows? By the time Justine has finished with us, we could be the next Fred Astaire and Ginger Rogers." He suddenly grabbed my waist and swung me around, sending us crashing into a group of students coming down the hall.

"Hey, watch it," one of the guys growled.

"Uh . . . maybe not," Chris admitted with an embarrassed smile. You couldn't help liking him. He was always the first to laugh at himself. I found myself hoping, for his sake even more than mine, that Justine could work a miracle and teach us to dance in one lesson.

Chapter 3

"This is so nice of you. I really appreciate this," Chris said over and over as we arrived at Justine's house. I could tell he was bugging her. He can't help it—he reverts to nerdy behavior when he's nervous.

"Right, let's get started," Justine said. "Help me move this furniture."

"Are you sure we should be dancing in here?" I asked doubtfully, looking around at the pastel silk furniture, the Chinese vases, which were probably worth a fortune, the ceramic lamps, and all the other stuff, which looked as if it had come straight out of *Lifestyles of the Rich and Famous.*

"It's the biggest room," Justine said. "I told my

31

dad we needed a house with a ballroom, but he wouldn't listen."

"Gee, what a mean father," Ginger said, giving me a dig in the ribs.

"Yeah, that's almost child abuse," I agreed. "I'd have left home if I couldn't have a ballroom."

Justine grinned. "Knock it off, you guys. We were looking at houses when I was about eight years old and we saw this one huge house with a ballroom. I really wanted him to buy it so that I could roller-skate inside. I always knew it would come in handy someday. This won't be easy on the carpet, but let's get started."

Chris and I kicked off our shoes and stood in front of her.

"Okay, let's start at the beginning," she said. "First position."

She turned her feet to impossible angles.

"Whoa!" Chris said. I hung on to him as he began to topple over.

"Okay, forget the positions," Justine said. "Let's start with pliés."

"Plee-ays?"

"Knee bends. We use them to limber up. Ready? Plié and up, plié and up."

We did this for a while.

32

"Justine, I hate to interrupt, but time's getting short here," I said finally. "I don't think the director will choose either of us because we have a great plié."

"We usually warm up for at least half an hour," Justine said, "but I can see your point. You have so much to learn. . . . Okay, let's move on to some of the floor moves. Jetés."

"Jay-tays?"

"It means 'to throw' in French. That's because we throw out the foot, like this." She did it, pointing out her leg and then bringing it under her again.

We tried. Chris jay-tayed to the right, I jay-tayed to the left, and we kicked each other.

"Ow," we both said, hopping around while Karen and Ginger laughed through their cheesecake.

"You guys are not taking this seriously," Justine scolded. "You look like the Two Stooges."

Chris and I were laughing now, and it was hard to stop. Everything Justine said seemed funny.

"Let's try the pas de chat," she said.

"Which means?"

"Step of the cat?" Chris asked, looking at me as he translated. We were in French class together.

"Correct," Justine said. "It's called step of the cat

33

because we spring lightly from one foot to the next, like this." She did it, very lightly.

We tried. It was impossible to decide when to lift which foot. Justine started laughing. "You guys look more like 'step of the elephant on hot sand,'" she said.

"This is hopeless." I sighed. "There's no way we're going to pick up real ballet stuff in one session. Couldn't you just teach us something that might make us look good and that's really easy?"

"Let's see," Justine said. "How about this?" She did a kind of step sway, step sway, turn, turn, turn.

We tried it. It was easy enough. Even I got it.

"Okay, Roni," Justine said, "now just don't plonk your feet down and don't look at your feet. Always stare straight ahead, arms out to the sides to balance yourself, and when you turn, your head whips around, like this."

She spun across the room like a top. We were very impressed.

"Wow," Chris said. "You mean like this?" He started spinning faster and faster.

"Help!" he cried as he headed, out of control, for the furniture. Justine and I leaped to grab him, but it was too late. He crashed into a tall floor lamp, which swayed and then started to topple toward one of the Chinese vases. Ginger and Karen did spectacular dives. Karen grabbed the lamp while Ginger snatched away the vase. The lamp missed by inches. We all looked at each other in horrified silence.

"Sorry," Chris muttered. "You didn't teach us how to stop. That was scary."

"Okay," Justine said. "No more turns."

"You know what I think?" Karen said carefully.

"What?"

"I think we should go outside to practice by the swimming pool where we can't do any damage."

"Great idea," Chris agreed. "I had no idea this dancing stuff was so dangerous."

"Neither did I, until now," Justine said.

"And you know what I think?" I said.

"What?"

"I think we should bring the cheesecake with us."

"Roni Ruiz, you have a one-track mind," Justine said, giving me a friendly shove.

Two exhausting hours later, I knew what a balancé was and how to do a chaîné turn and I could point my toes. But that was about it—hardly enough to make Baryshnikov come and seek me out as his next partner. Hardly enough to get me a part in a high school musical, either!

As I walked down the dirt road that leads to our house, I found my mood swinging between excitement and despair. In my wildest daydream I imagined the director saying, "Who cares whether you can dance or not, Roni Ruiz. You're the best comic actress in this school and we've got the perfect role for you."

Then reality would set in. I'd remember how I had managed to turn the step of the cat into the step of the elephant and I'd picture the director saying, "Sorry, but we need people who can dance without killing anyone."

I don't know why this play was so important to me, but it was. I suppose I'd been looking forward to it all year, ever since that senior had said he had big plans for Chris and me in the spring play. After we'd won the talent show, it was easy to believe him. The show had been the most amazing experience—kids I didn't know, and even teachers, had stopped me in the halls and told me how great I was.

I wanted that feeling again. I'd loved just being onstage. Before we went on, I was terrified, but once the audience started laughing, I completely forgot how nervous I was. I didn't want the scene to end, and I certainly didn't want the applause to end. I guess I'm just a ham at heart!

As I opened our front gate my dog, Midnight, and my little brother, Paco, both hurled themselves at me at the same time.

"Hi, Roni. Hi, Roni," Paco yelled. "You came home!"

The kid can be annoying at times, but it always makes me feel good to be greeted like this, as if I'd been away for years and not just a few hours.

"Whoa, you guys, you're knocking me over," I said, laughing. "Has Mama got dinner ready?"

"Mama's busy," Paco said. "She's running around the house like crazy, taking out all the furniture."

"She's what?"

"That's what she's doing," Paco said solemnly. "She told me to go play outside and she's making the girls do their homework on the patio, even though they keep telling her there's too many bees."

"What's all this about?" I asked.

He shrugged. "She keeps saying there's not enough room."

"For what?"

"I don't know." He skipped off happily, leaving

me to find out why my mother had finally flipped.

I opened the front door cautiously. He was right. The sofa had been pushed almost up to the front door and there were now two beds in the living room.

"Mama?" I called. I wasn't sure what to expect next.

She came out of the bedroom, smoothing down her hair with her hands, something she always did when she was worried. "Oh, Roni, thank goodness you're home. I need help here."

"What's going on, Mama? Is something wrong?"

"Plenty's wrong," she said. "How are we going to sleep eighteen people in this house? I keep trying to fit them in, but it doesn't work."

"Are we turning this place into a hotel or what?"

"It's not funny," she snapped. "I finally heard from your aunt Luisa today and they're all coming, even cousin Luis's family from Guadalajara."

"Coming here? What for?"

She looked at me as if I were crazy. "For your *quinceaños*, of course. How could we hold the celebration without all the family?"

I groaned. "Why do people I've never met have to come to my birthday party? I don't even want a big party. A nice dinner for my friends at a restaurant would be good—that's what Justine's parents did. Or we could have a barbecue at home."

She was looking at me as if I'd grown another head. "What are you saying, *hija*?" she demanded. "It's not up to you what you want. It's the custom— the family all comes, you wear a beautiful dress for the blessing at church, and then you are presented to the community at a big reception. That's how it's always been."

"But that's a Mexican custom, Mama," I said. "It was fine back in the old country, back in the old days when you couldn't wait to get daughters married off. This is America! Kids don't dress up like brides here. They don't do stuff like this. I'll look stupid. My friends will laugh at me."

"Your friends will be proud to celebrate with you, if they are true friends," Mama said solemnly.

"Mama, please," I begged. "I really don't want to do this. Can't we just have a normal party? Do we really have to invite a lot of relatives I don't even know?"

"Of course we do," she said angrily. "Everybody expects it. If your aunt Luisa had had girls instead of boys, we'd have gone down there for their *quinceaños*."

"Well, I'm not wearing one of those dumb dresses," I said.

39

"Of course you are," my mother cried, horrified. "You should be thankful that you have parents who are willing to put on a big celebration for you. When I was your age, my parents were so poor that—"

"That you all had to share one tortilla?" I teased. I could see right away that this was the wrong thing to say. I was only trying to lighten things up, but I guess my mother wasn't in the mood. A hurt expression came over her face.

"If you don't want to hear, fine," she said, and started straightening furniture.

I went up to her and put my arms around her. "Of course I want to hear," I said. "I was only kidding. What happened when you were my age?"

"My family was so poor, we couldn't afford a new dress for me," she said. "So I had to wear my cousin Consuela's. She'd had her *quinceaños* the year before, in the same village. As I walked down the aisle in church I thought everybody was whispering, 'Poor Dolores, her family is so poor that she's wearing the dress her cousin wore last year.'"

I had to laugh. "Poor Mama," I said. "I guess teenagers don't change much."

"At least you won't have that worry. We've been saving for the big day," she said. "Everything will be perfect. You'll look like an angel."

"That'll be a first for me," I quipped.

She smiled. "So now my big worry is where do we put them all?"

"Tell them to stay at a hotel," I suggested.

"Tell my family to stay at a hotel? What kind of people will they think we are? Family is family."

"Then borrow cots and put them on the patio," I said.

"Abuela will have to have a room to herself," Mama went on. I didn't see why my grandmother had to have a room to herself when everyone else was forced to play sardines, but Mama seemed certain. "And I can't put your boy cousins in with you and the girls."

"Are they cute?"

"Your cousins are fine boys," she said. "Fine young men. The family is very proud of them. Your cousin Carlos is going to be an engineer. He's a very nice boy." She frowned. "And when they are here, I don't want to hear any of that fresh American talk. They won't understand that you're just joking. They'll think we've really let our daughter run wild."

"I have one question," I said. "My birthday isn't for another month. Why are these beds in the living room right now?"

41

"I was trying things out," she said, "but there's no way I can get it to work. You'll have to help me . . . there's so much to be done between now and then. The bedrooms need new curtains and bedspreads. I'll have to start cooking right away—Mrs. Lopez says I can use her freezer. And then we have to choose a pattern for the dress and arrange with the dressmaker for fittings. Oh, no! And then there's the cake. We have to decide on a bakery. Maybe we'll have the reception at the church catered. . . ."

"Whoa," I said. "This is worse than a wedding."

"It's just like a wedding," she said, "only there's no groom to worry about. I'm counting on you, Veronica. I'm going to need your help from now until the big day."

I opened my mouth to tell her about tryouts the next day. If I got a part, I'd be kind of busy at school. But then I shut it again quickly. I knew what she'd say. She'd tell me not to go to tryouts.

I'll just try out for a small part, I told myself. *Just a few lines, or even the chorus if I can sing well enough. Nothing too demanding. My family has to understand that school life is important to me too.*

Then a terrible sinking feeling came over me. "Mama, when exactly have you planned this party?"

"Let's see," she said. "Your actual birthday is the

eighteenth. That's a Thursday, right? So the guests will arrive from Mexico on the Friday. We'll have a small party for the family on Friday night, your big party on Saturday night, and then you'll be presented at church on Sunday morning."

The weekend of the twentieth—that was just a few days before opening night of the play. How could I possibly fit a *quinceaños* into that schedule?

"Go put it on the calendar right now, Roni. I hope Papa managed to get the band I wanted."

I walked across the kitchen like a zombie. I knew I should tell her, but I couldn't.

Mama came up behind me as I was writing on the calendar.

"It's going to be your big day, *hija*," she said proudly. "I've been looking forward to this for so long. It will be wonderful, won't it?"

I managed to give her my biggest, brightest smile. "Oh yes, Mama. It will be wonderful."

Chapter

4

"I've got a big problem," I told Ginger as we got on the bus together the next morning.

"Oh, don't worry," she said. "I bet most girls haven't taken years of ballet like Justine."

"This is way bigger than my dancing," I said. "I might not even be able to be in the play at all."

"Why not?"

I looked out the bus window. The last of the fields near my house were giving way to the upscale new estates that were growing like mushrooms around our neighborhood. I kept on staring because I suddenly felt I might cry.

"It's my stupid birthday party," I said. "I knew it was coming up, but I had no idea my mother was going to turn it into a cross between a wedding and a Hollywood production. Our whole family is coming from Mexico. My mother is trying to fit eighteen people into our house, which she plans to redecorate totally before they get here. I've got to be fitted for a dress. Someone's going to have to bake three zillion enchiladas. . . ."

"You mean you might not have time for rehearsals?" Ginger asked.

"And my party is the weekend before opening night," I continued. "You can imagine what the last weekend will be like—totally crazy. I don't think the director will understand if I have to leave to go to church."

"I'm sure he would," Ginger said soothingly. "It is a big occasion, after all."

"He'll tell me I shouldn't have tried out if I knew I couldn't be there," I said. "Which I guess is true. But I really want to be in this play, Ginger." I turned to look at her. "What do you think I should do?"

"If it really means a lot to you," she said slowly, "then I guess you should go for it. After all, this party is your mom's idea, not yours. Tell her she'll have to fit her party in with your rehearsal schedule."

"Yeah, right," I said. "Can you imagine me trying to tell eighteen angry relatives that they'll have to wait until eleven-thirty for me to cut my cake? Or what the priest will say when I ask him to have my celebration mass at six in the morning?"

"It does seem like a big problem," she said. "And you don't even sound too thrilled about this birthday party."

"Thrilled? I hate it."

"Then don't do it."

"I tried telling my mother I didn't want the stupid thing, but she said I had no choice. She said it's our tradition. How come I had to be stuck with a family with all these weird traditions? Nobody's going to dress you up like a bridal Barbie doll for your fifteenth birthday."

"Anybody who tried to dress me like a bridal Barbie doll would die," Ginger said. "It took at least twelve years to get me to wear something other than jeans. But my dad would never make me do something I didn't want."

"My whole family expects it, that's the problem," I said with a big sigh. "They're all coming—half of Mexico is emptying out. I have to go through with it, whether I like it or not."

"It might turn out to be kind of fun," Ginger said. "You'll get loads of presents. Maybe there will be dancing and you can find yourself a cute guy."

"I guess it could be okay, if it wasn't right now," I said. "And if I didn't have to make a fool of myself in a frilly white dress."

Ginger snorted. "And this is a girl who actually wants a comedy role in the play? That's not making a fool of yourself?"

"That's different," I said. "When I'm up onstage, playing somebody else, it feels great. I know I'm not me and I can be as wild as I want. But I hate it when it's *me* people are looking at. Does that make sense?"

"Not really," Ginger said, "but I understand anyway. I've been your friend for so long that I can follow your weird logic."

"How does this logic sound," I said. "I was thinking that I should be reasonable and just go for a small part in the play. If I didn't have too many lines and I just appeared in a couple of scenes, it wouldn't matter too much if I wasn't there, right?"

Ginger patted my knee. "I can tell you really want this, Roni. I say go for it! And anyway, you haven't even been chosen yet. Maybe you won't get a part and that will solve everything."

"That's not the way I want it to be solved," I said.

The auditions were held in the auditorium after school. I promised Chris I'd meet him outside the door. He was a bundle of nerves, and he didn't want to go in there alone. I knew how he felt. My own stomach felt as if I'd just stepped into an empty elevator shaft. I waited by my locker for Justine to join me. She had decided to try out too.

"I feel it's my duty, Roni," she said when she informed me that she had to change into her ballet clothes for tryouts. "They need someone who knows what they're doing."

I was feeling so tense that I couldn't even come up with my usual squashing remark to this. I watched her as she headed for the locker room, so confident and bouncy. How could she go through life like that? At least she didn't have to worry about getting a dancing part. I bet there weren't many people who danced better than she did.

"Good luck, Roni," Karen called as she took out her homework books.

"Why don't you come too?" I suggested. "It might be fun if we were in the chorus together . . . and you too, Ginger." I grabbed her around the waist. "We could be a kick line—whoops!" I forgot that we were in a crowded hallway, and my kick caught a large guy in the rear end. He turned around and glared at me.

Ginger started laughing. "Roni, the secret weapon of the chorus line," she said.

"See, I need you to look after me."

"You don't. You'll be fine," Ginger said. "Besides, if they heard me sing, the whole place would empty in two seconds."

"And I have too much other stuff to do," Karen said. "Between tutoring and the newspaper, I don't have time. But I'll come to your opening night and write the review if you want."

"Only if it says that Roni Ruiz was the star of the whole performance."

"Depends how much you pay me."

"What kind of friend are you, anyway?"

It felt good to be kidding around like usual.

"Where's Justine?" I asked, dancing up and down nervously. If we waited much longer, I'd have to go to the bathroom again. "I wish she'd hurry up. Chris is waiting for me outside."

At that moment there was a sort of strange commotion down the hall—sort of a mixture of gasping and giggles. We looked in that direction and groaned. Justine was coming toward us, dressed like something out of the Bolshoi Ballet. She was wearing a pink leotard, pink tights, and pink satin shoes, and her hair was up in the sort of severe bun that ballerinas wear.

"Ready to go?" she asked brightly.

"Justine, why are you dressed like that?" Ginger spluttered.

Justine looked surprised. "It's a dance audition, so I wore my normal dance clothes," she said.

"But nobody else is dressed like that," I said worriedly.

"Then I'll stand out as the only professional, won't I?" Justine answered calmly. "Are you planning to dance in that awful T-shirt and shorts, Roni?"

"That's all I've got."

Justine sighed. "Maybe it's a good thing in your case. They're so baggy and shapeless that nobody will be able to see if you move well or not. Come on, let's go. You're going to make us late hanging around here talking."

She swept ahead of me down the hall, not seeming to notice that every single person did a double take as she passed. That's Justine for you. Roni, the famous "step of the elephant" dancer, followed behind in her shapeless baggy shorts, not feeling too happy.

I felt even less happy when I got inside the auditorium. There were thousands of kids trying out. Some of them were dressed in aerobic clothes, looking almost as professional as Justine. They were doing stretches while they chatted. Chris moved close to me. "There are a lot of kids here," he whispered. "I wonder how many parts there are."

"Not this many."

"I hope the other guys can't dance as well as those girls over there," he said. "Is this a big mistake, Roni? Are we crazy?"

"No way. We've been looking forward to this, Chris." I tried to sound more confident than I felt. "And it's no big deal. If we get picked, fine. If we don't, it's only a crummy high school play. Who cares?"

He gave me a weak smile. "I guess you're right," he said. "Can I ask you a big favor?"

"Sure."

"Try out with me. I don't want to go up on that stage by myself."

"We don't even know what we have to do yet."

"I know," he said. "I wish we'd prepared something. We could have been dynamite in a scene together."

"Were we supposed to have something prepared?" I was just realizing how little I knew about auditions.

"I think it's usual," he said. "And I bet we'll have

51

to sing something, too. Did you bring any music with you?"

"Music?" I looked longingly at the door.

"What songs do you know?"

"Nothing that I could sing onstage."

"Me neither."

We looked at each other and laughed. "Looks like we're doomed," I said. "We'll just have to wing it."

"Roni, I'm glad you're here," Chris said. "I'm glad I met you. I really think you're special."

I smiled at him. "I'm glad I met you too, Chris. I bet we're going to be just fine."

"Yeah," he said. "We'll get up there and—"

"Listen up, people," called a lanky black guy standing onstage. "I'm Greg Sanders, and I'm going to be the director, along with Mrs. Hammond from the drama department and Ms. Peters from PE. I'll let Ms. Peters talk first."

I knew Ms. Peters by sight, but I wasn't in her class. She looked all athlete, not an ounce of spare flesh on her. "Okay, people. I just want to say a few words before we start. *Oklahoma!* is a musical."

"No kidding—I thought it was an existentialist drama," whispered a voice from behind me. There were nervous giggles throughout the auditorium.

"And in a musical, everyone is expected to sing

52

and dance a little. We're going to start with dance tryouts. We don't expect *Swan Lake*, but we need to see who moves well and who doesn't. Let's start with the girls, because I know the guys are going to be self-conscious onstage." More laughs and groans. "So can we have all girls up onstage, in lines of ten."

I glanced back at Chris, who mouthed "Good luck" as I made my way up onstage with half the female population of Alta Mesa. I found a spot in a row near the back. That would give me time to pick up the steps before anyone noticed me.

"Excuse me, Ms. Peters, but there are eleven in the front row," I heard a girl call out.

With a sinking feeling, I saw that Justine had pushed herself into the middle of the front row. I was only glad she hadn't dragged me with her.

"She cut in," someone complained.

"I was only trying to be helpful," Justine said. "I thought the girls behind me might pick up the steps faster if they had a professional to watch."

Ms. Peters cleared her throat. "Why don't you . . . uh . . . step back a row, Sonia," she said to the girl beside Justine. "We get to see everybody in the end."

The girl glowered at Justine and made faces at her friends as she moved back. Justine sure had a knack for upsetting people. I knew I'd never push myself forward like that, even if I'd come straight from the American Ballet Theater.

"She has guts," the girl next to me whispered. "I wouldn't want to be on the wrong side of Sonia."

I nodded, not wanting to let on that Justine was my friend. I just prayed she wouldn't call out to me, or invite me to come stand beside her! As I looked around, I saw one girl who wasn't onstage. She was dressed in black aerobic wear but she was sitting near the piano, looking very relaxed.

"Who's she?" I asked the girl beside me.

"That's Annabel," she said reverently. "She's already got the lead. Greg precast the leading roles. She's had tons of experience and she studies voice."

"Who's the leading guy?"

"It was going to be Peter Hostetter—you know, the football player? But he just broke his ankle playing baseball, so now I don't know who they'll find."

Ms. Peters came up onstage. "This is a really simple routine, girls," she announced. "We'll start with a step sway, step sway, turn turn turn."

A big grin spread across my face. Justine was a genius. I'd actually practiced this one. I remembered what she had said about not looking at my feet and holding out my arms as I turned. Ms. Peters added a couple of steps as we went on, and I could do them too. I was feeling more confident by the minute. The front row danced, then they moved to the back, and so on. Finally it was our turn. I looked ahead, I pointed my toes, I held out my arms. I swayed and turned with everyone else. I was pretty good!

When all the rows had finished, the directors had a long discussion and then Ms. Peters came on-stage with a clipboard.

"We're going to ask the following girls to stay as members of the dance chorus," she said. "From these girls we'll assign speaking and singing parts later. These are just preliminaries for girls we know we can work with."

She started pointing to people. She pointed to Sonia, she pointed to Justine. She came to my row and she pointed to the girl beside me. Then she passed on.

I hadn't been picked.

Chapter

5

I was ready to burst with anger. How could they not have chosen me? I had been just as good as the girl beside me. I'd watched her. She hadn't even pointed her toes or held out her arms! A voice in my head whispered that I should be happy, because now my birthday problem was solved for me. But I didn't feel even a teeny bit happy. I wanted to be in this musical. I wanted it badly.

The stage began to clear. The girls who weren't picked drifted away, some of them muttering to each other. Those who were picked made their way down to the auditorium, trying to walk like dancers in a musical. I knew what Justine would have done right now. She'd have made a big fuss and demanded to know why she'd been overlooked. I looked at Ms. Peters's disappearing back and I tried to make myself call out to her, but my mouth wouldn't obey me. Maybe that was because I wasn't one hundred percent sure I *was* good enough. Secretly I was scared that Ms. Peters might shake her head and say, "Oh no, you didn't move well enough."

But I couldn't just give up and slink away with those other girls. Like I said, I'm a fighter. So I followed Ms. Peters down the steps to the auditorium. When she stopped to consult her clipboard, I took a deep breath and tapped her on the back.

"Excuse me," I said.

She turned around. "Yes, dear?"

"I think you forgot me."

She looked flustered. "Your name is?"

"Roni Ruiz."

She examined the clipboard in front of her. "I don't see . . . I'm afraid that you're not . . . ."

"But I was better than some of those girls you picked," I blurted. "I watched them. They didn't even point their toes. I know I'd be okay for the chorus."

She nodded. "I remember watching you," she said. "I thought I had you down . . . here it is! But

57

your name's been crossed off the final list. I don't know why."

Someone had crossed me off the final list. Someone was trying to spoil my chances of success. I had no idea who, but I wasn't about to take it. Roni Ruiz doesn't give up so easily.

"Just give me another chance," I said. "I know I can do this. I really want to be in this play."

Ms. Peters looked worried. "Greg?" she called. "I've got a young lady here who—"

She didn't have time to finish. Greg was heading in our direction. He took one look at me and a big smile spread across his face. "Roni, great, you're here," he said. "I've been looking for you. Where were you?"

"I was up there, trying out."

He grinned. "Why were you trying out for the chorus? I told Chris to tell you I had something in mind for the two of you. Come over here. I need to know if you can sing."

"I've never tried it."

"Never?"

"Only in the shower," I said.

"Then pretend this is the shower," he said. "What can you sing by heart?"

I tried desperately to think, and all I could come

up with was a McDonald's commercial and "America the Beautiful."

I started, timidly, "Oh beautiful, for spacious skies, for amber waves of grain . . ."

I sounded like a mouse squeaking. I could feel the flush creeping up my cheeks.

Greg held up his hand to stop me. "Way louder. Pretend you're alone in the shower."

"For purple mountain majesties, above the fruited plain . . ." I went on.

It was pretty clear I was no Whitney Houston. Greg stopped me right away. "I think we can work with that," he said, looking across at the two teachers for confirmation. "Now try this." He nodded to the pianist, who pulled out a piece of music and started playing.

"I'm just a girl who can't say no," Greg sang, "kissing's my favorite food."

He really hammed it up as he sang, fluttering his eyelashes and acting like a flirtatious girl. I started laughing.

"Now you do it like that," he said.

I tried. It wasn't a hard tune—I guess I must have heard it before on TV. And I'm great at hamming it up. Greg smiled. "Yeah, I think that will work well," he said. "Chris, get over here!"

Chris came across from the group of guys waiting to go onstage and joined us. Greg had us read some lines together. Then he talked with the two teachers for what seemed like an eternity.

"I had an idea when I watched you two together in the talent show," Greg said, turning back to us. "There's the lead couple in the play and then there's this other couple—Ado Annie and Will Parker. I wanted to try them really comic, almost slapstick, so that the play's not boring for kids. I think you two could do it. I have this great hoedown number in mind—you know, getting into a promenade and losing your partner, going the wrong way, swinging with the wrong guy, bumping into people. . . . It could be very funny. You think you could handle it? It will mean a lot of hard work."

I looked across at Chris. His eyes were shining.

"I can handle it," Chris said. "I'm prepared to do what it takes."

They were all looking at me.

"I—I don't know," I stammered. "I'll give it a try."

I couldn't believe it! I'd gotten a part in the school musical. And not just any part—a great part, a funny part, a part I was just dying to do.

Reality didn't set in until I was on the bus going

home. Greg had given me the script, telling me to mark it up and learn my lines as soon as possible. As I went through it, panic began to overtake me. Annie was in a scene with Laurie, the lead. Then there was a scene with the peddler man, then with Will, then she sang a solo. She had hundreds of lines. No, make that thousands. This was a really big part.

Of course I was excited—I was just a little freshman and I'd gotten the second lead in a big play. But a voice in my head was whispering that there was no way I could handle this and my birthday too. I should go to Greg tomorrow and tell him that I'd made a mistake and that I couldn't handle a part this size. Maybe he'd let me be in the chorus instead, and that would be fun. But I knew in my heart that I couldn't do it. I wasn't going to give up this part, even if it killed me.

My mother was waiting for me when I got home. The beds had disappeared from the living room, but every item of furniture was now covered with yards and yards of fabric.

"Roni, where were you? I wanted to get all this done before Mrs. Gonzales came over to measure you for the dress," she said.

"I had to stay late at school," I said. "Sorry. All what done?"

"You tell me," she said, waving at the fabric. "Which goes best in Monica and Carmen's room and which in yours?"

"I don't like any of them," I said, wrinkling my nose. They were the sort of bright flowery prints that my mother loved and had made me wear until recently.

"They're not for you, silly child," Mama said. "I want the rooms to look pretty for the guests. Now, your room is darker, so do you think the lighter one with the roses?"

"It's not going to be left in there after they go, is it?" I demanded. "I like my own lace curtains, and my plain comforter."

"Most girls would be grateful that their mother wanted to redecorate their room for them," she snapped.

"Sure, if I get a say in what goes in there. You know I don't like flowers. I never did."

"Flowers are suitable for young girls," Mama said. "Okay, since you won't decide, we'll put this in Monica's room. You can help me measure after school tomorrow. Right now we have to clear this away because Mrs. Gonzales is coming at five-thirty."

Mrs. Gonzales was a neighbor. I'd never liked

her too much. Her daughter Francisca was a couple of years older than me, and we had to play together when we were little kids. She used to dress me up as her baby and boss me around. I hated it.

"Why does Mrs. Gonzales have to make my dress?" I muttered.

"Because she's offered to and it would be rude to refuse."

"You can buy dresses in the store, you know."

"Yes, for two hundred dollars."

That made me shut up. I didn't want my parents to spend any more money than they already were. So I tried to be polite when Mrs. Gonzales arrived with her pattern book and tape measure.

"All skin and bones," she said when she measured me. "You don't feed her enough, Mrs. Ruiz. She may even have that, what do you call it, anorexia. People die from it."

My mother looked at me and laughed. "Roni has a healthy appetite," she said. "That's just the way she is."

"It will be harder to pick out a style for her." Mrs. Gonzales shook her head. "She won't fill the dress out nicely like my Francisca did."

I grinned to myself at this. Francisca Gonzales was a tall, chubby girl whose clothes were always

63

too tight. I wished Ginger had been there so that we could have giggled about her.

Mrs. Gonzales opened her book and started showing me patterns. "This is my favorite. It's what I made for Francisca," she said. It was a nightmare dress—worse than a bride on a wedding cake— with layer after layer of frills and lace and ribbons. I'd look like a giant marshmallow.

My mother caught my expression. Before I could say anything she interrupted quickly, "That's not really Roni, I'm afraid. She likes things simpler than that."

We went through the whole book. There was nothing I even liked.

"Couldn't I just wear white shorts and a white T-shirt?" I joked. "I'll wear a bow in my hair if I really have to."

Mrs. Gonzales looked at me as if I were crazy, and Mama frowned.

"Such a pity she cut off her hair," Mrs. Gonzales said to my mother.

Mama nodded and gave me a hard stare. She'd never forgiven me for getting my hair cut the day before school started. I really liked my short style, but I could understand that curls over my shoulders would have looked better with a formal gown.

In the end we settled on the least frilly dress, but it was still pretty gross. I expected it to look even grosser by the time Mrs. Gonzales had finished with it.

By the time I went to bed, I still hadn't told my family about the musical. I had to say it exactly the right way, or they'd freak out and tell me to quit immediately. I lay in bed, looking at my familiar lace curtains, which were soon to be replaced by big ugly roses, and decided that maybe I just wouldn't tell them. Ever.

I filled Ginger in on this as we sat on the bus together the next morning.

"How can you not tell them?" Ginger asked. "They'll wonder where you are all the time."

"I'll keep thinking of different excuses," I said. "Things they can't object to, like track meets."

"They must know track is over."

"I'll tell them this is the postseason."

Ginger rolled her eyes. "I think they'll guess there is no Super Bowl for track."

"So I'll think of something better. I figure if I'm incredibly cooperative at home and I help my mom bake and sew all night every night, then she's got nothing to complain about."

Ginger looked at me with concern. "Don't kill

yourself over this, Roni. You've got homework every night. You've got this huge part in the play. Something's got to give. If you get sick, then you can't do any of them."

"I know," I said. "Don't worry. I'm strong. I can handle anything."

I don't think she believed me.

Chapter

6

After school, Chris was waiting outside my classroom to escort me to our first rehearsal.

"Did you get many of your lines learned?" he asked.

"Are you serious? I barely had time to go through the script and mark it up."

"Greg said he wants us without books by the end of next week," Chris said smugly. "I spent three hours on it last night, after I was done with my homework. I think I know our whole first scene together. Do you want to test me and then maybe we can show Greg the scene?"

"I wouldn't mention that if I were you," I said. "Nobody else will know their lines yet and you'll look like a studious geek." Chris flushed and started to walk on ahead, hugging his books to his chest. I hadn't meant to be unkind, but he'd scared me. I'd hit back without thinking.

"I bet we don't even get to rehearse. There will probably be more tryouts today," I said, hurrying to catch up with him and make things better between us. "After all, he did tell people he picked for the chorus that some of them would get speaking parts."

Chris managed a weak smile. "That's right," he said.

Justine was already in the auditorium, doing stretches against the wall, dressed in yet another ballet outfit. This one was all white, and she was wearing one of those bows in her hair you see Russian gymnasts wearing. I could see a group of girls watching her and obviously whispering about her. Justine didn't even seem to notice. The truth was, they were probably jealous. It would have been hard to find fault with her. Even her stretches looked good.

Greg appeared with his clipboard under his arm. "Okay, gather round. Everyone ready to go?" he asked.

We gathered.

"I want to try out the chorus people in some of the parts we haven't cast yet," he said, "and then I'd like to do a complete read-through."

"How can we do a complete read-through?" Annabel drawled, looking down at her red fingernails as if she was totally bored. She wasn't wearing aerobic clothes today, but teeny white shorts and a black halter top. "Is there any point if I don't have my leading man yet? I can't act to myself."

"I think we might have solved that for you, Annabel," Greg said.

"You've found someone?"

"Maybe," Greg answered, giving her a mysterious smile.

"Not one of those geeks who tried out yesterday?" Annabel said loudly, throwing up her arms in mock horror. "They were all so terrible, darling. And none of them looked like a Curley. I'm not doing a love scene with any of them."

I looked at her with interest—and dislike. I'd never seen a prima donna up close. Since all the geeks from yesterday were here listening, I thought it was very rude of her. Chris was one of them, and I was angry on his behalf. I expected Greg to say something, but he just laughed.

"The guy I'm trying to get is not what you'd call

a geek, honey. He's not anyone's idea of a geek."

"Who is it?"

"He told me he'd be here if he decided he had the time to do it," Greg said. He glanced across at the door. "Hey, great timing. Here he is now."

We all followed the direction of his glance. In the doorway, framed against the bright sunlight, his curls glowing as if they were on fire, stood Drew. He grinned as everyone stared at him, gave an exaggerated celebrity wave, and came across the stage toward us.

"Okay, you convinced me," he said to Greg.

"Great to see you, man," Greg said, coming forward to grasp his hand. "This is a big favor you're doing us." He turned to Annabel. "There you are, Annabel honey. I told you I'd find a perfect Curley for you, didn't I?"

Annabel sort of oozed toward Drew. "Well, hi there," she cooed. "I don't think we've ever met, although I've watched you play football. You're Drew, aren't you?"

"And you're Annabel," he said.

"How clever of you to know that."

"Everyone knows who you are," he said. "You'd have to be blind not to notice you around school."

"Same goes for you," she said.

I glanced at Justine. She mimed putting her finger down her throat and making gagging noises. I giggled and felt a little better. Drew had to be hamming it up for our benefit. He couldn't really be interested in someone like Annabel, could he?

"Okay, people, grab chairs and form a circle onstage for the read-through. You too, chorus people. I'll assign parts as we go."

I picked up a chair and straightened to see Drew staring at me. "Roni?" he stammered. "What are you doing here?"

"I'm in the musical."

"That's great!" he said. "We get to act in the same play. What a blast!"

He was smiling at me, and all the old feelings came rushing back. His smile still had the power to make my heart start racing. It was incredible— every time I thought I'd gotten over Drew, I found that I was wrong.

Instantly Chris appeared at my side. "I saved you a seat, babe," he said. "You want to go through that scene while we're waiting?" And he slipped an arm around my shoulders.

Babe? Since when had Chris ever called me babe? I don't let anyone on earth call me babe. Drew gave me a half-amused, half-questioning look as Chris steered me away. He couldn't have been more obvious if he'd come right out and said, "This is my girl—don't mess with her."

The trouble was that I didn't want to think of myself as Chris's girl. I liked Chris. I enjoyed his friendship. He made me laugh. But I knew by now that he'd never make me feel the way Drew had.

As we found our seats I heard Annabel talking to Justine. "How does she know Drew?" she asked, pointing to me.

"They used to be an item," Justine said, in her too-loud voice. "But she dumped him."

"For the geek?"

"Hard to figure, right?"

If I'd been close enough, I would have kicked Justine.

We sat in a circle and read. Several things became instantly clear: Drew was perfect for the swaggering, sexy Curley. And Annabel was definitely making a play for Drew. She wasn't acting when she looked over the top of her script and said some of those lines to him. I tried to find it funny. Maybe Drew and I would meet up afterward and laugh about it.

He'd make some joke about his boyish charm being irresistible to all women, and I'd tell him he hadn't gotten any less conceited since we broke up, and then he might just say that he still missed me. . . .

"Roni, wake up, it's your cue," Chris said, digging me in the side.

At the end of the rehearsal, Greg asked Drew and Annabel to stay so that he could block a couple of scenes with them. Chris put his arm around me again. "You want to go get a soda?" he asked, loudly enough for everyone to hear.

"I have to rush home," I said. "I've got a million things to do." I was about to say "for my birthday party," but I shut up. I wasn't one hundred percent sure that I was going to invite Chris to my *quinceaños*. Sometimes I found him annoying . . . like right now.

"Oh. Okay," he said, and his face fell. Then I felt like a jerk.

"I really do have to rush," I said. "My mother's trying to redecorate my bedroom, and I'm supposed to be helping."

He smiled shyly. "Okay, see you, then. Get those lines learned."

I went in one direction and Chris in the other. How did he manage to make me feel so guilty all the time? I wondered. I just wished he wouldn't look at me like that. Why did he have to be so easy to hurt?

"Roni, where have you been again?" my mother demanded as I stepped into a living room covered with fabric. "You know how much there is to be done."

"Sorry," I said. "I had to see someone after school."

"Not detention?" she asked in horror. "You're not failing, are you?"

"Of course not. It was just that one of the teachers asked some of us to stay late . . . to discuss . . . things," I ended lamely. I expected her to demand what things we had to discuss and why only some students had to stay late, but she didn't.

"I can't be expected to do all this by myself," she said. "How can I cut and measure at the same time? How will these rooms ever get finished?"

"Anyone would think the Pope was coming for a visit," I grumbled.

"I don't want our family to think that we live like slobs," she said. "Now grab the tape measure and don't make any mistakes."

For two hours we measured and cut. Then I had

74

to help get the little ones to bed, and then there was homework. It was late by the time I finally got to look at my script. I bet Chris had memorized half of it by now. I tried to learn my lines, but they went right out of my head again.

I fell asleep sitting up in bed with my script on my knees, and I woke in that same position the next morning feeling stiff and uncomfortable. I moved like a zombie and had to sprint for the bus.

"So how did the first rehearsal go?" Karen asked as we met by our lockers.

Justine shrugged. "I had to sit there all afternoon for nothing. We haven't done any dance routines yet. And it's not fair! They gave all the good parts to Annabel's friends. I have exactly one line to say. 'Hurry up, Laurie!' That's it. That's my one moment in the spotlight."

"You'll have to make the most of it," Karen said. "You'll have to go, 'Hurry . . . up . . . Laurie.'" She accompanied it with grand gestures.

"You should have tried out, Karen," I said.

She shook her head. "No, thanks. I know what I can handle and what I can't," she said. "And right now newspaper, tutoring, violin, and school is more than enough. But I bet it was fun, huh, Roni?"

"I don't know about that," I said. "Drew showed up."

75

"Drew?"

"Yeah, he's going to be the leading man."

"Annabel's already throwing herself all over him," Justine said, laughing loudly. "Talk about unsubtle. She was so obvious, wasn't she?"

"Oh, yeah," I said.

Ginger glanced at me and frowned. "Is that a problem for you, Roni? Having to work alongside Drew, I mean?"

"Why should it be?" I said brightly. "That was all a long time ago. It will be fun working with him. Drew's a funny guy."

I could feel Karen looking at me as if she knew what was really going on inside my head. "I hope it is okay, Roni," she said. "I don't know if I could handle acting with James."

"Don't worry about me. I've had months to get Drew Howard out of my system," I said. "Besides, I've got Chris there, making sure everyone knows I'm supposed to be with him. And I get a feeling that Greg is going to be working us so hard that I wouldn't even notice if King Kong was onstage next to me."

"I hope this is as easy as you think, Roni," Karen murmured as we picked up our books and headed for our first classroom. "Drew was really special to you."

"Okay, so he was special. He was my first big

crush," I admitted. "My first real boyfriend. Guys like Drew don't come along often."

"Maybe this will be a chance for you two to get back together again," Karen suggested.

I shook my head firmly. "Forget it," I said. "It didn't work out the first time, remember? I just couldn't keep up with his lifestyle. Besides, I bet he'd never go back to an old girlfriend. That would be bad for his image."

Justine was still smiling. "Annabel doesn't seem to mind that she's a junior and he's only a sopho-more," she called to me. "Do you think their love scenes will get really steamy?"

I couldn't stand it any longer. Didn't she realize what she did to me when she talked about Drew and Annabel? "Shut up, Justine," I said. "It's only a musical. People just stand three feet apart and sing at each other."

"I always think that's so funny," Ginger said. "Can you imagine in real life if a guy suddenly looked at you and burst into song—"

"Hey, Roni!" I spun around at Chris's yell. Immediately he started singing, "With me it's all or nothing. Is it all or nothing with you? It can't be in between. It can't be now and then. No half-and-half romance will do."

He was singing, loudly, right in the middle of the hall. And what's more, there were nerds behind him. Everyone was looking.

The nerds applauded wildly. Other kids were clapping too.

"So what do you think?" Chris asked me. "That's our duet. I learned it last night."

"I think it's time we went to class," I said, giving a despairing look to my friends. I grabbed Ginger's arm and we hurried in the direction of the classroom.

I tried to concentrate on world geography, but I couldn't. I felt as if I was rapidly losing my grip on life as I knew it.

My shy, retiring boyfriend was now serenading me in the hall.

My gorgeous ex-boyfriend would be on the same stage as me every day for a month.

And somewhere in between, I had to go for daily fittings for a dress I hated for a party I didn't want.

Chapter

7

Drew was sitting on the edge of the stage, dangling his feet, as I came in to rehearsal that afternoon. With nobody near him, he wasn't putting on an act for once, and he looked like an adorable little boy. I longed to rush across the room and throw my arms around him.

"Hey, Roni," he called, his face lighting up when he saw me. Maybe Karen was right. Maybe there was still hope for us. I tried to remind myself that it hadn't been all roses with Drew before. He'd flirted with other girls. He'd wanted to do all kinds of expensive things on weekends, things like horseback riding and river rafting, which were way out of my budget. But he'd still been the most amazing thing that had ever happened to me.

I was only halfway to the stage when Chris came running to catch up with me. "Roni, wait up," he called, grabbing my arm and swinging me around. "Look, I wanted to apologize to you about this morning. I was just so proud that I'd learned the song. I wanted to show you. I hope I didn't embarrass you too much."

"It's okay," I said. "But please, in the future just sing on cue, onstage, and with no nerds around."

"Oh, speaking of nerds," Chris said, looking around cautiously. "I suppose I should warn you . . ."

"Out of the way, please. High-tech equipment passing through," came Owen's high, squeaky voice.

I looked at Chris in horror. "What are they doing here?" I mouthed.

"They're techies," Chris said. "Walter is writing a computer program to handle the lights and scenery all from one board."

They had drawn level with us now, four nerds holding a big box of goodness knows what.

"How about that magnificent solo?" Owen asked me, peering intensely through his heavy-rimmed glasses. "Weren't you impressed with the quality of his voice? The Pavarotti of Alta Mesa!"

"Owen, please shut up," Chris said, blushing

80

scarlet with embarrassment. Owen's voice was loud and bounced off the high ceiling of the auditorium.

Owen, as usual, wasn't sensitive to what upsets normal humans. He went right on, "You should have been given the lead, old buddy. Hey, let's tell the director that. Come on, Ronald, we'll do it right now. Make Chris the star he deserves to be."

"No! Thanks all the same," Chris yelped, looking at me for help. Sometimes the nerds got to be too much even for him.

I leaped to his defense. "Chris was telling me about your plans for the scenery and lighting," I said.

Four nerdy faces lit up. "You heard about Walter's brilliant scheme?" Owen asked. "All the stage manager needs to do is stand in the wings and press buttons. Backdrops will come up and down, curtains will open and close, lights will go on and off, and scenery will move, all thanks to Walter."

Walter shifted from foot to foot and grinned nervously. "It's really quite simple," he stammered.

"And we're here to install this masterpiece," Owen said. "Wolfgang's going to do the heavy work. Ronald and I will be supervisors. Right, Ron?"

"We will indeed," Ronald agreed.

"I've got a question, Owen," Walter stammered.

81

"Fire away, old buddy."

"When do we get to put this box down? My arms are about to drop off."

They staggered on toward the backstage area. Chris gave me an apologetic grin.

"If you say they mean well, I'll punch you," I threatened. I looked up to see other cast members watching us with interest. Drew was grinning, then he turned to say something to Annabel. Great, so now I was identified as a nerd groupie.

It wasn't what you'd call a smooth rehearsal. For one thing, as soon as we started blocking a number onstage, Greg's voice was drowned out with strange noises—hammering, something heavy being dragged, Owen's high-pitched shout as something landed on his toe, Ronald's loud demand, "What is this supposed to be and where do I put it?"

"Can we have some quiet back there?" Greg yelled.

Owen's head appeared through the back curtains. "Sorry, but you can't disturb geniuses at work."

"Shouldn't that be genii?" Ronald's voice cut in.

"Definitely genii. It's Latin," Walter added.

"Isn't a genii something that lives in a bottle?" Wolfgang's deep voice growled.

The whole cast now had that strange expression on their faces that my friends and I always had after dealing with the nerds—it was a look that said reality as we knew it was rapidly slipping away.

"Let's get back to business, people," Greg said, shaking his head in disbelief. "This first number involves almost the entire cast. Let's have the girls from the chorus across the stage in three rows."

Justine managed to get herself right in the middle of the front row again.

Ms. Peters took over. "This first number is very simple, and I'd like everyone to learn this routine, because we might use this same step sequence again," she said. "Let's start with step, behind, side, front, rock, rock. Got that?"

"Ms. Peters?" Justine asked. "Wouldn't it be smoother if we did pas de bourrée, balancé, instead of what you suggested?"

"I . . . uh . . . think we'll keep it simple, thank you, Justine," Ms. Peters said.

The routine went on. Every time Ms. Peters suggested something, Justine came up with something better. When she finally said that step swish, step swish should turn into pose, attitude, and maybe a cabriole thrown in at the end for effect, Ms. Peters lost it.

"Justine, this is not the Met," she yelled. "Most of these girls don't know a pose from a jeté. Now please stop trying to show off your ballet knowledge."

Justine looked offended. "I was just trying to make the routine better," she said. "It's kind of dull the way it is right now."

"Then it will have to stay dull," Ms. Peters snapped. "I have to teach five routines in a week to a group of kids, most of whom have never taken dance before. We don't have time for fancy stuff. This has to look good for a performance four weeks from now."

She turned her back on Justine and started going through the steps again. By the end of the session everyone had gotten the hang of the number, and we tried it with music.

It was clear right away that there was going to be a problem. Everyone else was going step, step, step, but Justine was doing all sorts of ballet moves, flinging out her arms and making sure her toes were pointed. She even tried a couple of the turns on the tips of her toes. When the chorus had to kick up their heels, hoedown style, Justine was doing jetés.

"Ms. Peters, Justine keeps hitting me," Sonia called out.

"I'm just doing the correct arm movements." Justine sniffed. "If you did them too, we wouldn't keep bumping into each other."

I saw Ms. Peters give Greg a despairing glance, and then they whispered together for a while. At the end of the number Ms. Peters said, "Justine, would you please come over here?"

My heart was in my mouth. Justine was going to get kicked out of the chorus for being too good. It was her own fault, I knew. She should have been smart enough to take her dance down to the level of everyone else. But I knew how upset she'd be. Even though she boasts a lot, she's not really as confident as she makes out.

I watched until Justine nodded and started to walk away. She seemed to be taking it very well. I ran over to her.

"What did they say?"

"They said I'm too good for the chorus," she said. "I stand out too much, which was pretty obvious, I suppose."

"Gee, I'm sorry," I said. "It's not your fault the others don't know how to dance."

"Oh, don't worry about it," Justine said, giving me a big smile. "They're going to write in a solo for me, during the dream sequence. What did I tell you, Roni? True talent always gets noticed and appreciated in the end. If I'm going to do a solo, I think I'd better go home and call the Phoenix Ballet. Maybe they'll let me take some classes with them to get back in shape. Maybe I can borrow their ballet master for a few private lessons. I wonder who I can get to design my costume? Well, gotta run! Enjoy."

And she danced off the stage, leaving me totally breathless.

We went through the rest of the rehearsal. I thought it went pretty well. In my scene with Annabel and Drew, I definitely got the laughs. And when I said some of my funny lines, I could see Drew looking at me in that special way.

"You're pretty good at this," he said to me as we came down from the stage.

"You're not so bad yourself."

We stood there for a moment, smiling into each other's eyes. I could feel my heart beating fast. Then he gave one of his famous cocky grins. "Yeah, I think I'll make a pretty cool Curley. Of course, the part was practically written for me."

"That's true. Curley's a conceited flirt," I suggested.

"He's a great-looking guy who has a way with

women," Drew countered, raising an eyebrow.

"Get outta here," I said, laughing.

"Can I help it if I have all the qualities of a star?" he said, laughing with me. Then he was suddenly serious. "You know, Roni, I thought being in a musical was a very uncool thing to do." He stared at me hard. "But now I'm glad I let Greg talk me into it." I got the feeling that part of the reason he was glad was that I was there.

Greg called us all over and started handing out rehearsal schedules. "You'll notice we open on Wednesday the twenty-fourth," he said, "so I want you to keep the weekend before that completely free. I get the feeling it will be nonstop rehearsals all day, and then we've got our first dress rehearsal on Saturday night. We'll make that our preview night for family members. Then two more dress rehearsals Monday and Tuesday, and then . . ."

He was still talking, but I wasn't listening. It was bad enough that there were going to be nonstop rehearsals all weekend. But Saturday night was the night of my big party, for which hundreds of relatives were flying in from Mexico. Now I really would have to tell my parents about the play.

✦　　✦　　✦

I was a nervous wreck all the way home. I loved being in the play. I'd dreamed about it, but I never thought it would be like this. I never thought that I'd be one of the stars. I never dreamed that I'd be onstage with Drew beside me. The whole thing was like a miracle. And if my parents didn't understand, then it would all vanish.

My mother was in a good mood when I walked in. "Your meet was over just in time," she said. (I'd told her we had a track meet tonight. I was running out of excuses.) "Mrs. Gonzales will be here any moment with the dress. And I've got wonderful news."

"We won the lottery?"

"Almost as good," she said cheerfully. "I just heard from my cousin Inez. You probably don't remember her. We haven't seen them since you were very small and we went to stay with them down in Mexico City. Anyway, she said they just got my invitation and of course they're all coming to your *quinceaños*. Isn't that wonderful? You'll get to see your cousin Alfredo again."

"Who?"

"You don't remember him either, I suppose," she said. "But when you were four and he was six, he fell in love with you. He told everybody he was going to marry you someday." She laughed. "You were so sweet together, holding hands." Then she looked up slyly. "You could do worse, and he's only a third cousin."

"Mama, please," I said, rolling my eyes.

"All I meant is that it can't hurt to make his acquaintance again. Show him around Phoenix. Introduce him to your friends. He's a fine boy. His mother is so proud of him—straight A's at school and a tennis champion. She says he's a great dancer, too. You two can dance together at the party!"

I had to stop her before she decided that my *quinceaños* dress could also double as a wedding dress in the near future. "So do you have any pictures of these cousins I don't know?" I asked.

"Oh yes, we've got pictures somewhere," she said. She went to a drawer and got out photo albums. As she leafed through them she showed me every other member of the family. Great-Aunt Rosa, who was now dead, so presumably wouldn't be coming. Aunt Luisa, Uncle Francisco, Cousin Carlos, and then finally she said, "Oh, here they are. This is Cousin Inez and her family."

It was only a small snapshot, with several people all crowded together, but at the front of it, squatting down, was a very large boy, a human blimp. He made Wolfgang look positively skinny. And he was scowling in an unfriendly way. This was my dream cousin?

"*That's* Cousin Alfredo?" I asked.

"That's him. A lovely boy," she said.

My brain was working fast. If there was one thing I couldn't handle on top of the play and my birthday, it was hanging out with a big, mean guy I hardly knew.

This is a job for the Boyfriend Club, I thought. *Not to set me up with the guy of my dreams, but to help me stay away from the guy of my nightmares!*

Chapter 8

I decided to wait until my father got home before I brought up the subject of the play. He didn't lose his cool as quickly as my mother did, and I didn't think he was into the *quinceaños* thing as much as she was. And what's more, I was his little princess.

Mrs. Gonzales came over and I tried on the dress. It was terrible—frill over frill. I looked at myself in the mirror and I saw the Bride of Frankenstein. But both my mother and Mrs. Gonzales were oohing and aahing. "Just adorable. She looks like an angel. She'll break hearts." I couldn't believe they were talking about me, or about the same dress. I stood there while Mrs. Gonzales pinned and tucked, my mind on more important things—like how I could state my problem so that my parents would understand.

"It's a pity you didn't arrive home a little sooner," Mama said to Papa as she began to serve dinner. "Mrs. Gonzales brought the dress for a fitting. Roni looked like an angel."

"She looked like a bride," Monica said, digging Carmen in the ribs and making her giggle.

"She looked stupid," Carmen said. At least one member of the family had good taste.

"You like your dress?" Papa turned to me.

What could I say? I shrugged. "I couldn't really see with it on me," I said.

"And good news—Inez is coming with the whole family," Mama went on. "Flying in on Saturday morning. They've already booked a hotel—a fancy hotel downtown. Of course, with their status it's only right, and Inez knew we didn't have the room. Now I'm worrying about the family party we're planning for Saturday. Do you think it will be too crowded here? Should we rent a hall for Saturday as well as Sunday?"

"A hall for Saturday night? Isn't that getting expensive?" my father asked.

I knew I had to say something fast. They had to know about my Saturday plans before they rented the Phoenix Civic Center and asked the Boston Pops to fly in. "Look, before you go on, there's something you should know," I blurted.

There must have been something in my voice that made them all look at me.

"I didn't tell you sooner, because I was afraid everyone would get upset," I said. "But the truth is that I haven't been staying late for teacher conferences or track meets. I've been staying at school because I'm in the school play."

"Roni, that's wonderful. Congratulations," Papa said, clapping.

"You're right, Papa. It *is* wonderful," I said, giving him a big smile. "And it's a huge honor, too. It's unusual for a freshman to get a big part in a school play, but the director chose me because he liked what I did in the talent show. I have one of the leads. I get to sing solos and everything."

"Our daughter's going to be a star, Dolores," Papa said, still beaming.

This was going too smoothly. "But there's a big problem," I went on hesitantly. "The play opens the week after my *quinceaños*. I thought that would be okay." (Not exactly true.) "I thought I could handle both of them." (Not exactly true either.) "But today I found out that the first dress rehearsal is on the same Saturday night as our family party."

"Then you'll have to tell them you can't be there," Mama said, folding her arms in the way that means, "I've made up my mind and you're not going to change it."

"But Mama, I have to be there. I told you. I have one of the biggest parts. They can't do the play without me."

"Then they must cancel their rehearsal," Mama said.

"They won't do that. They have to have dress rehearsals."

"Then you must tell them that you've changed your mind and you can't be in the play."

"Not be in it? But it's the chance of a lifetime, Mama. You don't understand."

"You're right, I don't understand," she said angrily. "What is more important, your family or a part in a play?"

I didn't think I should give her an answer to that one. Instead I turned to my ally across the table. "Papa, you understand, don't you? They offered me this big part in the play and it was like a dream come true. How was I to know that it would be on the same night as my party?"

I got up and went around to him, wrapping my

94

arms around his neck. "I really do want to do this, Papa. I can't back out now. We've been practicing too long." (This wasn't really true either, but it sounded good.)

Papa nodded. "It seems to me that this play is a great honor, Dolores," he said. "It's important that she does well in school. Who knows, maybe she'll turn out to be a great actress."

My mother didn't stop frowning. "She always was good at being dramatic," she said. "Every time she got a splinter, I thought it was a scorpion bite."

"But your mother is also right," Papa went on, making me hold my breath. "Your family is important. Your relatives are paying a lot of money to fly here for your celebration. You want them to arrive here and then we say, 'Sorry, but there's no party'?"

"Of course not," I said. "But there will be the mass on Sunday, and then the party afterward, and . . . and we could hold the party for the family on Friday instead! They'll all be here. And Friday is closer to my real birthday."

"We could do that, Dolores," Papa said, but I could tell it was a question. He wanted her approval.

"Friday?" Mama said. Then she sighed. "I suppose we could have it on Friday. But what about

Cousin Inez and her family? They are not arriving until Saturday."

This was an added benefit! If I could pull this off, I would have one less social occasion with my cousin, the bad-tempered blimp.

"You can bring them to my play on Saturday," I said excitedly. "You can bring all the relatives. The director said we could invite family."

"We could do that," my father said. "Think how proud they'll be to see our daughter onstage."

I could tell my mother was torn between giving in on this and sticking to what she believed was right. At last she sighed again. "I suppose we could do that, and hold the party on Friday. It will be harder for you, José. You'll have to entertain all those people as soon as you get home from work."

Papa smiled. "They'd be here anyway. We'd still have to feed them and entertain them. So now we kill two birds with one stone."

I flung my arms around his neck again, almost squeezing him to death. "Oh, thank you, Papa." I ran around to my mother. "And thank you! You don't know how worried I've been about this. And I promise I'll help you as much as possible, Mama."

"That's good to hear," Mama said, "because this week I start baking. Will you be here?"

"Of course, Mama. I'll help you every moment I'm not needed for rehearsals."

She nodded, and I realized I'd won.

"So what is this play, Roni? Tell us all about it," Papa said.

I perched on my father's knee and started to tell them. It felt as if a great load had been taken off my back. I was going to manage the party and my play after all.

What I hadn't counted on was more problems the next day at school. The day started just fine. I grabbed my friends as soon as they arrived at their lockers and told them the terrible story of my cousin, the blimp.

"I'm counting on you guys," I said. "You've got to find a way to protect me from him. If he went around holding my hand and saying he was going to marry me when he was six, imagine what he'd do now."

They were all trying not to laugh. "Maybe he's not as bad as he looked in the photo," Karen said kindly. "People often look unfriendly when they're frowning into the sun."

"And maybe he's not as fat as he looked," Ginger added. "Maybe he was cold and he was wearing layers."

97

"It was on a beach and he was wearing a T-shirt," I said. "He was totally gross. I don't see how my mother could like him."

"Maybe he has a wonderful personality," Karen said. She's our resident optimist.

"Then you can dance with him at my party," I said, "and you can volunteer to show him around Phoenix for me. In fact, you could pretend that you're me, and that would solve everything."

Karen and Ginger were already laughing when Justine said seriously, "But I don't see how that would work, Roni. Won't he notice that Karen's Asian American?"

Justine stood there saying, "What? What did I say?" for about ten minutes as we laughed at her.

We were still laughing when we went to English class. Mrs. Epstein waited for quiet. Then she said calmly, "Before we continue our discussion on Emily Dickinson, I just wanted to remind everybody that the research paper I assigned at the beginning of this quarter is due on the nineteenth. You should have all your information collected by now, so you can begin arranging it into the final paper."

From the way students were looking at each other, it was pretty obvious that most people were about as far along as I was. They hadn't even found a topic.

"No sweat," I heard someone behind me whisper. "We've still got three whole weeks."

I felt as if a cold, clammy hand were gripping me. When would I have time, during the next three weeks, to write a research paper? I knew it was totally impossible.

After class I went up to Mrs. Epstein. "I have a big favor to ask," I said hopefully. "I wondered if I could get an extension on that paper? You see, I have a lead in the school musical and my big fifteenth birthday party is coming up then too, and I just don't see how I can handle all three."

She wasn't smiling this time. "You should have thought of that and completed it earlier, then," she said. "I'm sorry, Roni, but a birthday party doesn't sound like a good excuse to me."

"But you don't understand. It's my fifteenth birthday and—" I wanted to explain to her what a big deal this was in my culture, but she waved her hand and interrupted me. "I don't care if it's your ninety-ninth birthday. You had plenty of notice for this paper and I'm not taking any excuses."

I left the classroom in a daze. Why hadn't I started the paper the day she assigned it? I bet

Karen had her information neatly on three-by-five cards by now. The topic was to choose a writer and show how that writer's body of work was influenced by his or her life and times. Maybe I could find a poet somewhere in the library who wrote only one short poem and died at nineteen. *Or maybe he died at almost fifteen of stress and overwork!* I thought ruefully.

"How far have you gotten on your research paper?" I asked Ginger on the way out to lunch.

"Are you kidding? I haven't even decided on a topic yet," she said.

"I need to find someone who had a very short life," Justine said.

"And was dyslexic so he couldn't write much," Karen added.

"I bet you've done most of yours," I said to her.

"Not most of it. I've just got notes on index cards. I haven't actually started writing."

See, I knew it.

"I thought I'd have plenty of time," I said. "But how am I going to manage it with the play and the party? Mrs. Epstein wouldn't give me an extension."

"Simple," Justine said. "Find someone and pay them to write it for you."

For once her totally stupid ideas didn't sound so bad. If I knew someone who would write my paper for me, I'd have paid them my entire savings!

Chris grabbed me as I went into rehearsal. "Did you get your lines down yet?" he asked.

"Almost." Big lie. I had learned scene one on the bus.

"You know it's without books on Monday," he said. "You better get your act together on this, Roni."

"What are you, the official slave driver?" I demanded.

He gave me an embarrassed grin. "Sorry. I didn't mean it to sound like that. It's just that I want you to be great in this play. I want both of us to be great. You want to come over to my house this weekend and we'll go through it together? Maybe right after Saturday's rehearsal?"

It did sound like a good idea. "I'd really like to," I said, "but I'm not sure if I've got time."

"You have to make time, Roni. This is important."

"I know," I said, "but I also promised to help my mother this weekend."

"With what?"

"Baking." It sounded so lame. "She has a couple of hundred enchiladas to make."

He was looking at me as if he wanted to read my mind. "You're choosing enchiladas over me? You're not trying to tell me something, are you?"

"Like what?"

"Like you don't want to work with me?"

"Of course not. It's the truth. Ask my mother. She'll tell you I'd rather be anywhere else."

He shrugged. "I just wondered if you were giving me the brush-off. That you might have . . . other ideas in mind." As he said this I could hear Drew's loud laugh. He sauntered into the auditorium, surrounded by a whole bunch of people. Drew was always in the middle of a crowd.

As I watched Drew, Chris suddenly pulled me into his arms. "I just thought we could work on our love scenes at my place," he said in a very loud stage whisper. "You know, get in some real practice."

"What are you talking about?" I said, pushing him away. "We don't have any love scenes. We sing."

"We could put some in," he suggested.

"What's gotten into you?" I asked, even though I could already guess. "Stop acting like this. You're embarrassing me."

He moved away a step. "It's just that this isn't working out how I imagined," he said simply. "I thought the play would be great. I thought we'd be together all the time and it would be wonderful."

I rested my hand on his arm. "I'm sorry," I said. "It's nothing to do with how I feel about you. I'm just overwhelmed, I guess."

"Then you should prioritize, like me," he said smoothly. "Make lists and give everything a time slot. That way you don't have to get into a panic."

Boy, you could tell what being around nerds had done to him. Sometimes I wondered why I liked him at all.

"Yes, but . . ." I began. Then I shut up. He probably had his research paper already finished. And how would he understand about trying on dresses and rearranging rooms for a dumb party?

It seemed like no one understood me, or my culture, or my problems. Why couldn't I just have a normal life, like everyone else?

Chapter

9

On Fridays my friends and I usually made plans for the weekend. I looked forward to weekends—we had so much fun together. We always tried to get together for a sleepover on Saturday nights. That had become our tradition since the school year started. And we did other fun stuff too—hiking or lazing in Justine's pool or just window-shopping at the mall. But this weekend was hanging over me like a big black cloud.

The others were already in mid-discussion when I came running out of the building to join them.

"Don't tell us you were kidnapped by the nerds again?" Justine said as I flung myself down on the warm grass.

"Or were you having another fight with Mrs. Epstein?"

"None of the above, but equally stressful," I said. "I've been talking to Chris. Again."

"Chris is stressful? How come?"

"He's turning into the biggest pain," I complained. "Ever since this play started, he's been bugging me nonstop. He thinks he's so wonderful because he's learned all his lines, and he thinks I'm terrible because I haven't, and he keeps on talking about professionalism and getting organized. At rehearsal yesterday, he gave me a speech about prioritizing. And today he thinks I should've followed his advice and everything would be just super. Plus, he's starting to act like a big shot onstage. You know—make way for the star!"

"Chris?" Karen asked in disbelief. "Shy Chris? The one who apologizes for everything and blushes when you talk to him?"

"You better believe it. But it's worse than that. He obviously feels threatened by Drew, so he's acting like macho man. He keeps grabbing me and giving me little kisses between scenes."

"It's true. It's disgusting," Justine said. She's always thought that Chris was too nerdy to be my boyfriend.

"And all the time I get the feeling that Drew and Annabel and all the others are watching us and laughing."

"Obviously he does feel threatened about being in the same play as Drew, so he's trying to make sure that everyone knows you're his girl," Karen commented.

"Yes, but I'm not his girl."

"You're not?"

"No! I mean, I like Chris, or rather I *liked* Chris. I liked doing stuff with him. We had fun. But I've never thought about him like . . ."

"Like Drew?"

"Exactly."

"So what are you going to do?"

"I don't know," I snapped. "I'm having enough trouble just getting through the day without sorting out my personal relationships. Can we talk about something else?"

"Fine," Ginger said. "We were just trying to help."

"There's nothing anyone can do, except for spiriting me into a parallel universe for the next month."

"I'm sure Walter could manage that," Ginger said.

"Don't talk to me about Walter, please. Do you know what it's like to have nerds around all the time on the set? Just when I think I'm looking cool onstage, Owen and Ronald appear and start talking to Chris and me like we're actual friends. It's hopeless."

"If you don't like the play, Roni, you can still quit," Justine said. "It's early enough to find someone else for your part."

"Of course I like the play," I snapped. "What a dumb thing to say. Can we change the subject, please?"

"We were talking about the weekend," Ginger said awkwardly. "So whose house are we going to?"

I looked up from the peach I had started eating. "For what?"

"The sleepover, dummy," Ginger said.

"Count me out," I said.

"Roni! You're going to miss the sleepover? We don't have rehearsal on Saturday night," Justine said.

"No, but Saturday night is the only time I've got to learn lines and do this dumb research paper."

"But, Roni, you need some time off. We always get together for our sleepover. It's traditional," Karen said.

107

"The whole world won't fall apart if I'm not there," I growled. "It's no big deal."

"Well . . . what about our other plans, then?" Karen asked, cautiously this time.

"What other plans?"

"You know, we talked about going shopping to look for dresses for your party?"

"Yeah, Roni, you have to come and tell us what's suitable," Ginger added.

"Look, guys, can't you get this straight? I don't even have time for the important stuff right now. I certainly don't have time for unimportant stuff like shopping or sleeping over."

"Well, sorreee," Justine said. "We didn't realize how unimportant we were. We'll just shut up and get on with our own little lives."

Ginger was frowning at me. "You were just complaining that Chris was acting like a big shot. Sounds to me like Roni might be the one who's acting like a star."

I jumped up. "That's totally untrue and unfair! Can I help it if I've got a million things to do that are more important than going to a mall? I've got rehearsals. I've got to help bake a million enchiladas and hang new drapes *and* Chris keeps bugging me about going through our scenes together in my spare time *and* there's the small matter of a research paper I haven't even started. And you guys are mad at me for not going to the mall? Some friends you are. You don't understand. Nobody understands!"

I snatched up my stuff and ran off, fighting back tears. I didn't talk to them all Friday afternoon, and nobody called me that night, so I guessed they were still mad at me. I supposed they had every right to be mad. When I thought back over what I'd said, I did sound like Annabel, only worse.

I spent a miserable night. I hate fighting with anybody, especially with my best friends. It didn't seem fair. How could the thing I'd always dreamed of turn into such a nightmare for me? When I thought of the next three weeks, I just wanted to go to sleep and wake up to find they were over.

Instead I woke up to the smell of frying onions and chili peppers. I looked at my clock—seven-thirty. I pulled on my robe and staggered into the kitchen. My mother was standing there with huge steaming pots all around her, looking like a witch in her kitchen.

"Why are you starting so early?" I asked.

"How am I going to get it done, if you're running off to your rehearsal at nine-thirty?" she asked. "I had to start early."

"I'll help now," I said. "What do you need me to do?"

"You spoon and I'll wrap," she said. So for the next hour I put big spoonfuls of the chili chicken mixture onto tortillas and Mama dipped and rolled them. When the trays were full, we wrapped them and put them in the freezer. We did almost a hundred enchiladas before I looked up and saw the time.

"Oh no—I'm going to be late! I haven't even showered yet. I'll miss my bus," I yelled. "Do you think Papa would drive me?"

"He left early to referee a soccer game," she said.

"I'm doomed," I muttered as I rushed into the bathroom for the world's quickest shower, then sprinted to the bus stop. Of course, the nine-thirty bus had left, so I had to wait for the ten o'clock.

The cast was in the middle of a scene when I crept into the auditorium. I prayed that it was a scene that didn't include me. I could probably have tiptoed in without anyone noticing, but Chris spotted me and yelled, "Here she is! Where have you been, Roni? We've all been waiting for you."

The whole scene stopped and everyone watched me walk down the auditorium.

"Sorry," I said. "I missed my bus."

"Overslept again," Chris said as he came to meet me. "She has a terrible problem waking up in the mornings, don't you, honey? But don't worry, Greg. I'll try and keep her in line for you from now on."

I couldn't believe what I was hearing. "Excuse me?" I demanded, giving him my coldest stare. "What are you saying?"

"Just a little humor to lighten up the situation, so you don't get in trouble," he said. He slipped his arm around my waist and pulled me close to him. "You really do have to shape up, you know. We had to change the schedule because you weren't here. You have to get serious about this, Roni. Start acting like a professional."

"If you don't watch it, I'll start acting like a professional boxer and land you one on the jaw," I said. "And if you must know, I've been up since seven-thirty and I've already made a hundred enchiladas."

"Well, sorry," he said, "but it really doesn't look good to show up late to our first Saturday rehearsal. Especially when you're one of the leads. We have to set an example for the little people, you know."

"The little people?" I repeated incredulously.

"You know what I mean," he said, blushing as he moved away from me.

"Okay, since Roni's here we can work on that

hoedown scene," Greg called. "Chorus, we need you onstage now."

He put us all in our places and started walking us through a complicated square dance. I was supposed to arrive in the middle of the number, carrying a basket of goodies on my arm, like Little Red Riding Hood, and get swept up into the dance. Greg handed me a prop basket.

"Now, everyone starts to promenade right. Roni, you pass between the first two couples and you grab Steven's hand. He twirls you around, you start to lose your balance . . ." He went on, firing directions at me. My head was spinning and it was hard to concentrate. The smell of those chilis was still in my nostrils, I was hot and sweaty from running from the bus stop to school, and I was mad at Chris for his dumb macho behavior.

"Now you wheel around to the right," Greg said.

I wheeled and caught Drew right in the back of the head with my basket. Instead of making a fuss, he turned around, a big grin on his face. "Oh no," he said, covering his head with his hands as if he expected further attacks. "It's happening again! It's all coming back to me. Flying books, flying chili, and now this."

"I'm really sorry," I said, smiling because I re-

112

membered all those other occasions all too well. How could I forget that I had met Drew because I'd hit him on the head with my French book and then thrown chili all over him by accident?

"It's okay," he said. "Just don't do it when the basket's full."

We went on with the scene. When we stopped for a break, I found Annabel standing beside me.

"I remember who you are now," she said. "I remember my cheerleader friends talking about this klutzy freshman who nearly killed Drew. Do you have a coordination problem or what?"

"Accidents happen," I said, fighting to keep my cool.

"Well, if you're trying this to get Drew's attention, I wouldn't bother," she said, smiling sweetly.

"It worked last time," I said.

I saw her eyes narrow. "Listen, klutz," she muttered under her breath. "Drew might have been interested in you once, because he likes novelty. But you're old news now. You're history. And he has better things to attract his attention."

"You?" I said, and I burst out laughing. "Drew can spot a phony a mile away."

She raised her perfectly painted eyebrows. "If it's a contest between you and me, then frankly, you don't stand a chance . . . even if your geeky little friend would let you out of his sight for a second," she said. "And I don't think *that's* going to happen."

She was right. Even as she was speaking, Chris appeared, his eyes sweeping the backstage area for me. When he spotted me, he pointed, and to my horror he snapped his fingers at me. "Roni, get over here," he called. "I want to show Greg that little number I've got worked out for us."

"See what I mean?" Annabel said smugly. "I'd stick with him if I were you. You two are so right for each other."

I couldn't think of a spectacularly witty answer to this, so I let Chris lead me away. But I was ready to explode any second. As if she had a chance with Drew! Drew liked fun, interesting people, not phonies with long red fingernails and too much makeup. And if I ever got a chance to escape from Chris's clutches for a second, I'd show her who would win the contest!

I managed to get through the rest of the rehearsal. I even stayed behind with Chris and Greg while we worked on a couple of our scenes together. The truth was, I didn't want to hurry home. Home meant another dress fitting, more enchiladas, hanging drapes I didn't like, and pretending to be as excited as my mother was. And all I had to look forward to after that was a boring Saturday night, working on an English paper and trying to learn lines. Not even any friends to sleep over with.

Secretly I would like to have taken up Chris's offer to learn lines together, but I didn't want to encourage him. I still couldn't get over the way he'd acted today. He'd actually snapped his fingers at me! That's how you call a dog, not a person! I had to let him know that he wasn't going to treat *me* that way.

It was hot by the time I got off the bus and walked down our street. I imagined how that kitchen would feel now, if Mama was still cooking. Neither Paco nor the dog was outside to greet me as I pushed open the front gate. I was supposed to be the star of the *quinceaños* extravaganza and nobody cared enough to meet me when I got home!

The front door was open. As I stepped inside I heard a strange laugh coming from my bedroom. Neither of my sisters laughed like that. Now I was really mad. My mother had brought in a stranger to help decorate *my* bedroom. Unless a relative had arrived almost three weeks early and I had been turned out of my room to sleep in the doghouse!

"Okay, what's going on here?" I demanded, striding into my room. Then I stopped with my mouth open. Karen was standing on a stool, while Ginger and Justine were fighting to hold up a curtain rod. They all looked at me with big smiles on their faces.

"Good timing, Roni," Justine said. "We need a fourth person here. It keeps falling down on Karen's head."

"Only because you keep letting go of it too soon," Karen said, rubbing her head.

"What are you guys doing here?" I stammered.

"What does it look like?" Ginger said. "We're the Save Roni Brigade. We've already chopped onions until we cried, folded empanadas, and now we're hanging drapes."

"But why?"

Karen got down from her stool. "We felt really bad about yesterday, Roni. We didn't realize how stressed you were. We didn't know how big a deal this birthday was to your family. But you never talk to us like that, so we figured you must be trying to do too much."

"We thought we could go to the mall any old time," Ginger added.

"I don't know about that," Justine cut in. "If I

116

don't go to the mall once a week, I get withdrawal symptoms. But I sacrificed for you, Roni."

"Well, you just got here an hour ago," Ginger pointed out. "It's not *that* big a sacrifice."

"Can I help it if the play needed their star dancer at rehearsal?"

I looked from one smiling face to the next. "You guys are the greatest," I said. "This is so nice of you."

"What are friends for?" Ginger said. "Although if I'd known I'd have to chop a zillion onions, I might not have come. I've only just stopped crying. Are my eyes still red?"

"What did my mother say when you showed up? Was she surprised?"

"At first," Karen said, "but then she said what nice friends you had. She's asked us to stay to dinner. Your dad's going to barbecue ribs, and we thought we could have our sleepover here. We can help you learn your lines."

I felt tears well up in my eyes. Five minutes ago I had been mad and depressed. Now I had a whole fun night with my friends to look forward to.

"You guys get the best seats opening night," I said, wiping a tear that had managed to escape anyway.

"Of course," Justine said. "I already told them that. They're coming to watch my dance solo, which will steal the whole show, of course."

I picked up the unhung curtain that was lying on my bed and threw it over her head.

Chapter

10

Late that night we lay on sleeping bags in the living room and watched the moonlight come in through the open windows. It was a beautiful night. We'd started out sleeping on the patio, until Justine thought she felt something wriggling inside her sleeping bag. Then we all got paranoid about snakes. When Midnight brushed his tail over Karen's bare arm, we must have woken the entire neighborhood with our screams. So then we'd gone inside, but we were all too uptight to sleep. Me especially. I felt like a juggler in a circus with ten balls in my hands. I went back over the events of the day. Annabel, Drew, enchiladas, and especially Chris. . . .

"So what am I going to do about Chris?" I asked.

"It depends what you want," Ginger said. "If you want to use this as an excuse to break up with him, then tell him he's being a pain and he'd better leave you alone."

"But I don't want to hurt his feelings," I said. "I know how sensitive he is, and I know his ego needs boosting."

"It's been boosted too much already," Justine said. "Any guy who snaps his fingers at you needs to be put in his place."

"But don't you think that was an act?" Karen said. "He feels unsure of himself, he sees Roni flirting with Drew—"

"I was not flirting with Drew," I interrupted. Then I remembered how we had stood there, our eyes teasing each other. "Well, maybe just a little."

"He sees Roni with Drew," Karen went on, "and he feels he has to take command of the situation somehow. So he does it badly, but his message is clear. He doesn't want to lose you, Roni."

"So what do I do?" I asked again. "I don't want to be mean—I do like him as a friend. But he's got to shape up."

"Then I think the answer would be to stop making him feel threatened," Justine said. "If you pay attention to him and make him think he's the greatest actor in the play and an all-around wonderful guy, then maybe he'll calm down."

"You may be right," I said. "It's worth a try."

"The question is," Karen said slowly, "what are you going to do about Drew?"

"What do you mean?"

She sat up, the moonlight falling on her hair. "Oh, come on, Roni. It's obvious you're still crazy about him."

"Okay, I admit it. But that doesn't mean I want to get together with him again. I can drool over movie stars, but that doesn't mean I'd actually want to date them—well, maybe one date with Brad Pitt. And anyway, this is a stupid discussion, because I'm sure Drew has never gone back to an old girlfriend."

"But you think he might still be interested, right?" Ginger said. "You told me on the bus that he was flirting with you."

"What about Annabel?" Justine demanded. "She's still coming on to him, right?"

"Like a speeding locomotive," I said. "But I really don't think she's going to get anywhere. I mean, Drew has good taste." I was going to say "He picked me, after all," but my friends got in first.

"Then why did he date you?" they all asked in unison.

"Shut up," I said, whacking each in turn with my pillow. They grabbed their own pillows, and soon we were in the middle of such a good pillow fight, I forgot all about Chris, Drew, and the play.

On Monday, I tried to put into practice what Justine had suggested. I was very sweet and attentive to Chris.

"You were so good in that scene," I said, taking his arm as he left the stage, "and I'm amazed at the way you've learned all your lines."

"You've either got it or you haven't," he said, smoothing back his hair. "I was born to act."

Okay, so this wasn't exactly going according to plan. Maybe my friends were right. Maybe he'd already had his ego boosted enough.

As the week went on, I began to suspect that we'd created a monster. Chris was getting to be more of a pain every day—and not just to me. He started correcting other actors about their lines:

"Hey, Annabel, you skipped a line there."

"What does it matter? It was only a couple of words."

"It mattered to the playwright or he wouldn't have put it in the script."

"Get lost, Chris."

"Just trying to make sure this play is professional."

You can imagine this wasn't going down well with the cast. It wasn't going down well with Greg, either. I don't think we got through a single scene without Chris stopping us with a suggestion for making it better. He was worse than Justine! Greg was polite at first. But as the rehearsals went on, it was obvious he was beginning to lose his cool. By Friday, it seemed as if he couldn't take it anymore.

"Whoa, Greg. Hold everything. I've just seen how we could make this fantastic!" Chris cried. "We change this into another dream sequence and have everyone move in slow motion. Maybe we can wear strange costumes and makeup to show it's a dream."

"Chris. Just say your lines on cue and shut up."

But he didn't shut up. When Greg told someone what they were doing wrong, Chris had to add something too.

"You should cool it, you know," I whispered after a really tense scene on stage. "Everyone's getting mad at you."

"Can I help it if I'm the only one around here who wants to make something of this play?" He sniffed.

123

"Everyone wants to do their best, Chris. They just don't see things the way you do."

"Maybe that's because I have more vision," he said. Then he grabbed my shoulders. "Don't you see what's happened here, Roni? I've finally found where I belong! I have a total feel for the stage. I know what I'm suggesting is the right thing for the play, but everyone is too stupid or lazy to listen."

"Maybe your ideas would be perfect if we had a Hollywood budget and six months to rehearse," I said, "but we go in front of an audience in two weeks and we've only just got the routines learned."

"I've been meaning to talk to you about that," he said. "You never do the same thing twice in that 'All or Nothing' routine. Sometimes you lift both arms up, sometimes only one. That number could be great if you'd just concentrate and stop being sloppy."

That was enough. "Well, gee, I'm sorry, Mr. Director. I'll try to do better next time," I said sarcastically.

"I'm sure you will," he said, giving me a big smile. "I'm counting on you, Roni. Don't let me down."

I tried to think of something crushing to say, but all I came out with was "Huh." My friends were definitely right. Chris's ego did not need any more boosting.

When I started to walk away, he pulled me back. "Hey, babe, what about tonight? We haven't spent any time together since this play started. It's time we had a few quiet moments alone." He put his arms around me in a kind of Hollywood clinch. He was about to kiss me—right in front of the whole cast! I stamped hard on his foot.

"You've turned into the world's biggest jerk, Chris Kennedy," I said as he hopped around holding his toes. "I'd rather spend a few quiet moments with Dracula."

He walked away as if he didn't care and started turning his charm on some of the chorus dancers. They all found an excuse to get away. I felt sorry for him, but I was angry too. I'd tried talking to him and it hadn't done any good. If he made a fool of himself now, it was his own fault.

Almost immediately, Greg called Chris and me onstage to go through our duet again. We started off, and Greg stopped us.

"This is supposed to be light and sweet. You're being overdramatic, Chris. Lighten up, make people laugh."

"I don't see it as a funny number," Chris said.

"It's tragic in a way. This girl's been cheating on her guy. No wonder he's mad at her. He's giving her a warning—it's me or nothing." I got the feeling it wasn't the play he was talking about.

"It's a funny number, Chris," Greg said. "That's how I want it played. Roni's doing it just great."

"Roni never does it the same way twice," Chris said. "That's why it's so hard for me to pick up the vibes. She's never focused enough."

"She looks fine to me," Greg said.

"That's because you're too easy on us all. You're letting all this sloppy stuff get by. You should get input from other people—it would make the end result better."

Greg's eyes narrowed, but he kept his cool. "I'm the director, and you play it my way."

"I'm only trying to help," Chris said with a shrug. "You could use some help. This thing is only two weeks away from performance and it's still total chaos."

"If you don't like it," Greg said in a voice that sent chills down my spine, "it's not too late to get out."

"Get out?" Chris demanded. "You're asking me to quit? I'm the only one who seems to know what he's doing around here."

"You might be good, but you're not indispensable, you know," Greg said. "I could take one of the chorus boys and put him in your place tomorrow. There's still time."

Chris's face was bright red now. "Fine. If that's how you feel, I will quit," he said. "I didn't like working with a bunch of amateurs anyway."

He stormed offstage and we heard the outside door slam behind him. For a second nobody moved. Then Greg said, "Okay, let's rehearse something else, since we obviously can't do Roni's scene anymore."

"But you can't just let him go," I said to Greg.

"He was getting to be a big pain," Greg said.

"But he really loved being in this play. It did wonders for his ego."

"I'll say," Greg said. "That guy had the biggest ego problem I've ever seen."

"You don't understand, Greg," I said. "He was a nobody. He hung around with those nerdy guys who are doing scenery and lights. Now suddenly he's good at something, and I guess it just went to his head. He doesn't really want to quit."

"Then he'd better come back with a changed attitude and apologize," Greg said.

I grabbed his sleeve. "Let me talk to him," I

127

said. "I bet he's feeling really dumb already."

Greg looked at me, confused. "Why are you sticking up for him? I didn't see him treating you very well."

"I know," I said, "but I'm the only friend he's got. If he comes back, will you give him another chance?"

Greg placed his hand over mine. "Okay. For your sake, I'll do it. You two work well together—or you used to work well together until Chris turned into the Phantom of the Auditorium. He's pretty good, but don't tell him I said so. And you're pretty good too, Roni." He squeezed my hand. "Okay, go do it. I hope you can make him see sense."

I hurried out of the auditorium and stood in the empty quad outside. I had no way of knowing where Chris had gone. On a whim, I went around to the bike racks. And there he was, sitting on the steps leading up to the school, staring out across the street and hugging his knees as if he was cold.

"Chris?" I called quietly.

He spun around. "What are you doing here?"

"I wanted to talk to you, before it was too late."

He shrugged. "It *is* too late. I've already blown it, haven't I?"

I went over and sat on the steps beside him. Even though they were in the shade, the concrete was still warm. "I can't believe it, Roni," Chris said in a small voice. "I wanted to be in this play so bad, and now it's over."

"Whose fault is that, Chris?"

"Oh, I know," he said. "I don't know what came over me. It was like I was possessed—I could hear myself saying things and it was like someone else took over my body."

"You can say that again," I said. He looked up and saw that I was grinning. He gave me a weak smile in return.

"I've been a jerk, haven't I?"

"Yes. You have been a jerk."

"What got into me, Roni? I've never been like that before."

"Stardom went to your head," I said. "It's happened to better people than you."

"You're right," he said. "I knew I was good, and I wanted the whole play to be as good as I was."

"That's just it," I said. "Not everybody is as talented as you. Greg's doing his best with a mixed bunch of kids and short rehearsals. You were acting like we opened on Broadway next week."

"I know," he said. "And now it doesn't even

matter, because someone else will get my part. Did Greg assign it yet?"

"No," I said. "I asked him to wait until I'd talked to you. He promised me he'd give you another chance if you came back with a new attitude."

"He did?" Chris's face lit up, then fell again. "I couldn't do that. Everyone would make fun of me if I came back. I bet they're making fun of me already. Let's face it. I'm finished."

"That's up to you," I said. "Greg thinks you're pretty good. He thinks we work well together. And I want you to come back. Who cares what the others think?"

"Y-you want me to come back?" he stammered. "But I acted like a jerk to you, too."

"No kidding," I said. "But in spite of what you might think, I really do care about you, Chris. We've been good friends for so long. It seems a pity to blow it over one dumb play."

"You mean you still like me?"

"As a friend," I said quickly. "I like you as a friend, Chris. It can never be more than that."

There was a long silence. Traffic droned at the end of the block. A plane came in to land at Sky Harbor. Then Chris said, "It's him, isn't it? Drew Howard. I knew it the moment I saw you

130

two together. You still like him, don't you?"

Then there was another long pause before I said, "Yes, I guess I do."

"So are you going back to him?"

"He hasn't asked me. He hasn't even given me a hint that he wants to get back together."

"But I've seen him look at you," Chris said. "He looks at you like he's still interested. That's why I got so scared. I knew I was losing you and I didn't know what to do about it."

I turned to him and put my hand gently over his. "Let's face it, Chris. There never was that special something between us, was there? We started out as good friends and that's all we've ever been. And is that so terrible?"

"No," he said. "Good friends is okay, I guess."

"Then let's stay good friends forever and ever, even when we're both famous Broadway stars."

"Okay," he said, smiling now. "So what do you think I should do, Roni? Should I go back to Greg right now?"

"I'd wait until tomorrow. Give him a chance to cool down, and then you can tell him you're sorry in private," I said. "That way you won't have the whole cast staring at you."

He nodded. "That sounds good. I'll do it.

Thanks, Roni. Thanks for everything."

"My pleasure," I said. "You don't think I wanted to do that duet with one of those geeky chorus boys, do you? None of them can even sing."

I stood up and held out my hand to pull him to his feet. "Go on, get out of here, and I'll see you tomorrow. I promise I'll try to get my movements down in that duet."

He held on to my hand. "You're special to me," he said. "I wish it could be different. I guess Drew Howard just has something I'll never have."

"Drew Howard isn't the ideal boyfriend," I said. "He made me unhappy when we were together. He's a terrible flirt. He loves being the center of attention. He spends money like water."

"Then why do you want him back?"

I shrugged. "You can't choose who you fall in love with. Drew was the first guy I ever loved."

"Then I guess I'd better wish you luck, Roni. I hope you get back with Drew and you're happy with him . . . and if you're not, I'll still be around."

I flung my arms around his neck, almost knocking him off balance. "See, I always knew you were a super-nice guy," I said.

Chris just smiled sadly as he went over to his bike.

I ran back across the school yard, feeling hopeful and excited. I hadn't wanted to listen to my heart until now, because I hadn't wanted to hurt Chris's feelings. But it was true—I had missed Drew Howard every day since we broke up. Nothing was the same without him. And now it was like Chris had given me his blessing.

I paused in the shade of the walkway between buildings, wondering how I should let Drew know how I felt. Should I come right out and tell him, or should I drop little hints and let him know by the way I looked at him? I decided to tread carefully. I didn't want to blow my chances by coming on too strong. Drew hated girls who chased him.

I could tell by the clomping noises and loud music coming from the auditorium that the final chorus number was being rehearsed. Silently I pushed open the door leading backstage and tiptoed up the steps. It was so dark after the bright sunlight that I could hardly find my way. I didn't see the figures in the shadows behind the backdrop at first. But then I heard a strange noise that made me spin around.

As soon as I saw them, I wished I hadn't. It was Drew and Annabel, and they were standing in the half-darkness backstage with their arms around each other, kissing.

I don't know how I got out of there. I turned and ran blindly back down the steps and didn't stop until I was safely out in the warm sunshine. I was so angry and hurt that I thought I might explode any second. How could he? She was the world's biggest phony, and he hated phonies. What was wrong with guys? Did their brains cease functioning whenever girls were around?

I clutched at the iron walkway support to stop myself from running back in there and tearing out Annabel's perfect curls. Then, as I calmed down, I told myself that this was a lucky break for me. Any guy who could be taken in by someone like Annabel wasn't good enough for me. I reminded myself that this wasn't the first time he'd been taken in by a cute phony, and I remembered all the pain I'd gone through back then. Drew was immature and not capable of appreciating a real girl. I was better off without him.

But I didn't feel better off. I felt as if I had a big hole where my insides should be. And I felt like a fool, to think that I'd really believed he still wanted me, when all the time he was just being polite and friendly.

"Okay, this is great," I told myself. "Now I have no worries about guys at all. I can concentrate on

134

being the best actress in this play and writing a killer English paper and having the best *quinceaños* in Arizona."

I smoothed back my hair and put a big, false smile on my face. Then I made a grand entrance, flinging open the stage door and walking loudly up the steps.

"I'm back, Greg," I said, loud enough for everyone to hear. "I hope I didn't delay the rehearsal. Let's get to work!"

I was proud of myself. I really was a great actress.

Chapter

11

After that, Chris couldn't have been more focused during rehearsals. And I was the most focused person there—never missed a cue, never needed telling twice. I was so focused that I never even looked at Drew. Whenever he headed in my direction, I was immediately busy somewhere else. One day he made a joke and looked at me with that dazzling smile. "I'm the world's worst kidder," he said. "Roni will tell you."

"Whatever," I said, and walked away.

He came to catch up with me. "What's with you?" he asked.

"With me? Nothing, nothing at all," I said, although his hand on my arm unnerved me more than

I liked to admit. "Why don't you go back and impress all those other girls? They can't wait to tell you how wonderful you are, but I really don't have the time."

He squeezed my arm. "Talk to me, Roni. Have I done something to upset you?"

"You can't upset me anymore," I said. "I just don't care. Whatever you do is fine with me." Then I broke away from him.

He didn't try to talk to me alone after that, but I got the feeling he was watching me when he thought I wasn't looking. I refused to think about it.

Outside of rehearsals I was a busy little bee. I studied my scene notes on the bus going home. I worked on my English paper—I'd decided to do it on Robert Frost. He was easy to figure out. He lived in the woods and wrote about them, so I actually understood his poems, which was more than I could say for most poets we had to read. I even stood patiently while the Bride of Frankenstein dress took shape around me.

The big day drew closer. I helped my mother make enough beds for a visiting army. I would have to share Monica's bed, which was one of my least favorite things in the world. She always makes it very clear that it's her bed, and she even draws a line down the middle and yells for my mother if I cross it. Then she flings her arms around and moans in the middle of the night. In case you wonder why I didn't share with my other sister, she still wets the bed sometimes. Enough said.

"I could always sleep over at Ginger's," I suggested.

Mama shook her head. "The family has come to see you. What would they think if you slink away every night?"

"And what will they think when they see me in church with giant bags under my eyes from no sleep all weekend?"

She ruffled my hair. "You do make a big fuss about nothing, *hija*," she said. "When I was your age . . ."

"I know. You had to sleep six to a bed, like sardines," I quipped.

This time she laughed and told me I was terrible.

At school the play was finally shaping up. Backdrops were painted. Scenery appeared and nerds scurried around, dragging cables and tripping over things. I was dying to see what the result of all their weird work would be. People knew their lines and dance steps. Sometimes we got through a whole scene without Greg stopping us. As I watched Annabel, I could see why Greg had chosen her. She had a wonderful voice, way better than the rest of ours. She could hit the high notes like an opera singer and she knew just how to behave on-stage. It didn't mean that I hated her guts any less, but I could admit she was good. When I heard her silly giggle behind the curtains, I always imagined she was there with Drew. But I kept my cool. I was proud of the way I was holding up.

I managed it right until my birthday. I'd almost forgotten what day it was, until I got to school and found that my friends had decorated my locker with crepe paper and streamers and a huge Happy Birthday balloon. Inside was a plate of doughnuts with HAPPY BIRTHDAY written on them in frosting. It took me completely by surprise—I had to press my lips together so that I didn't cry in front of everyone in the school hallway.

"We're giving you presents at your party on Sunday," Ginger said, "but we wanted you to have something special today."

"This means a lot to me," I said. "My family decided that we'd celebrate my birthday tomorrow night, at the family party, and my mom's making a special dinner tonight, but that's not the same as getting up and finding presents and cards."

That put me in a good mood all day. Then Chris brought flowers to rehearsal.

"Happy birthday," he said shyly.

"That is so sweet of you. How did you know?"

He looked pleased and embarrassed. "A little bird told me," he said.

"Thanks, Chris," I said. I stood on tiptoe to give him a kiss, which made him blush bright red.

When Annabel saw the flowers, she frowned. "I guess you don't know, since you're not really an actor. But you don't get flowers until opening night," she said.

"Can I help it if my fan club can't wait?" I said sweetly.

Greg called us together and warned us to be patient because this would be our first trial run with full lighting, scenery, and props. He told us not to get scared if bits of scenery started moving by themselves or spotlights shone on us. It was all part of the famous computer program.

It didn't take us long to discover the hazards. A haystack appeared onstage in the middle of the first dance number and freaked out the dancers. Annabel was dazzled with a sudden spotlight and forgot her lines. (I enjoyed that part.) Then, in the third act, there was a great yell of horror behind the curtains. I knew that yell. It was Justine.

"You have got to be kidding! I don't believe it," she screamed.

I hurried in her direction. She was dancing around in front of Greg, and there were no jetés and steps of the cat. She was stomping—a spectacular temper tantrum. I doubt Annabel could have done better.

"This is an insult. Do you know how hard I worked on this number? Do you know I'm the one quality dancer you've got?"

"Calm down, Justine," Greg was saying. He looked frightened. "I know you're good, and the dance number is perfect."

"Then why isn't anyone going to see me?"

"It's a dream sequence," he explained weakly.

Justine looked up and saw me. "Do you know what they're trying to do?" she yelled. "They want me to dance behind a gauze screen while Annabel sings. All you see is my silhouette. I could be anybody. Nobody will even know it's me."

I tried not to smile, because I knew I'd be mad too, but it was just typical of things that happened to Justine. She always wanted to be the star, but something always happened to get in her way. This time it was a thick gauze screen hung over the entire stage.

"They'll still be able to admire your dancing, Justine," I said, "and they can look in the program to see who it is."

"Thanks a lot," she said. "I can just see them all scrambling to get their programs in the total darkness, trying to find out who I am."

"Let's run through your dance now, Justine," Greg said. "The lighting on that gauze still isn't right."

She glared at him. "With my luck the lights will all be on Annabel and nobody will even know I'm there."

"That's why we're going to get it right now," Greg said, putting a friendly arm around her. "Cheer up. You're our only dance soloist."

We finished the last act. It was absolute chaos. Greg must have thought so too.

"We need another tech rehearsal," he said. "Those scenery changes just aren't working yet, and the lighting is terrible. I can't use our first dress rehearsal to get this kind of stuff right—we'll have an audience, and I don't want us to look bad. We'll just have to have a tech run-through tomorrow night."

"Tomorrow night?" someone else yelled before I could. "But that's Friday night, Greg. I have a date."

"And I have a big party," I said.

"Look, I'm sorry, guys," Greg said. "I know you all have other things to do, but we have to do this. I did tell you to keep the final weekend free, so no excuses. I want everybody here at six. If you work well, we'll be out of here by ten."

Ten o'clock, on the night of my family party? Somehow I didn't think they'd understand. I went up to Greg. "Do you really, really need me?" I asked. "All my relatives have come into town for my party. My mother is going to be so mad."

"Sorry, Roni," he said. "You're too important. Your solo was one of the problem lighting cues. You'll have to tell your folks that you're sorry, but you have to be here."

I walked out in a daze. I could imagine how that would go down with my parents, especially my mother. Some of the relatives would have arrived by now and be sitting in our dining room when I had to break the news. I wished I didn't have to go home.

When I got home, it was worse than I'd imagined. The house was full of strangers. Little kids I'd never seen before ran up and grabbed me, yelling, "Hi, Roni." Mama came to rescue me.

"This is Ramón and Lupe, Cousin Consuela's

children. Come meet Cousin Consuela, Roni. And your *abuela* is here." I hugged strangers and then I gave my grandmother a big hug. At least I knew her.

My father came home and we all managed to squeeze around the dinner table. Everyone talked so much, I didn't have to say anything.

"So much food, Dolores. Are you sure this isn't the party food you're using up now?"

My father laughed. He was enjoying playing host. "This is just a simple supper. You wait until you see what she has cooked for tomorrow. Tomorrow will be a feast, right, Roni?"

I managed a weak smile.

"Is there going to be a band?" Cousin Carlos asked.

"For the big celebration on Sunday. Tomorrow is just family and close friends."

"But we have to have a band," Uncle Somebody boomed. "It's not a party without a band. The young ones need to dance. The old ones need to dance too!" He laughed loudly. "You find us a band who will play tomorrow night, José, and I'll pay. My treat."

This was getting to be too much. Now a band would be playing for a party I wasn't even attending.

I waited until my mother started clearing the table, then grabbed some dishes and hurried after her.

"Mama, I have to speak to you. It's very important," I whispered.

"What is it?"

I glanced back into the dining room. Everyone was talking and laughing loudly.

"About tomorrow night. Can we make it a late dinner? You know how people in Mexico like to eat late."

"That's true. Shall we say dinner at eight?"

"I was thinking more like ten-thirty."

"Ten-thirty? Are you out of your mind, child? Why would we want to wait until ten-thirty to eat?"

"Because I won't be there until then."

"Not be there? What are you talking about?"

"Mama, don't be mad, please, but the director said that we've got to have an extra rehearsal. He wouldn't listen. He said no excuses."

"No excuses? Your whole family here from another country and that's not an excuse?"

"I have a big part, Mama. They can't do it without me."

"They'll have to do it without you," she said, "because you're not going."

"Mama, I have to! I can't let them down."

"Are you trying to tell me that a stupid play comes before family?"

"Just this once."

"Then I haven't brought you up the way I hoped," she said. "I'm disappointed in you, Veronica. Your relatives are not wealthy people, but they've all paid to fly here for your celebration, because family is important. We've switched things around once to try and fit in with your schedule, and now you've changed it again."

"I'm sorry," I said. "There's really nothing I could do."

"You could have turned down this play in the first place if you knew it would cause such heartache. You only think of yourself. I've worked hard to make this a special occasion, and now you pretend it doesn't matter."

"I know it matters, Mama," I began, but she shook her head angrily.

"You make fun of the dress, you have no time to help me prepare, and now you won't even attend your own party. What kind of daughter is that?"

My father appeared in the doorway. "Is something wrong?" he asked.

I looked at him hopefully. "Papa, she's mad at

me because I have an extra rehearsal tomorrow night and I'll miss most of my party."

My father's eyes shot open in surprise. "Miss your party? Impossible. Your mother and I have worked hard on this. We're proud you're in a play, but enough is enough. I'll go to your school tomorrow and explain that you had a prior commitment to your family."

"No, Papa. You're not coming anywhere near my school," I said. "You don't understand. There are a lot of kids in the play. I can't let them down. I'm going to that rehearsal, and you can't stop me. You'll just have to go on with the party without me. I never asked for this dumb *quinceaños* anyway!"

"Veronica!" my mother gasped in horror.

Before she could say anything else, I ran out of the kitchen. "Here's our birthday girl," one of my uncles said, trying to grab me. I fought free and rushed into my bedroom. It was only after I'd slammed the door that I remembered it wasn't my bedroom anymore.

And it was only after I'd stood there for a while in the darkness that I remembered today was my birthday.

Chapter

12

I escaped to school early the next morning, so that I didn't have to face all those angry relatives. Karen greeted me cheerfully as soon as I crossed the school yard.

"Has your large cousin arrived yet? I need to know what duty I'm going to be assigned."

I shook my head. "He gets in tomorrow."

She looked at my face. "Roni, what's wrong?"

I told her every horrible detail of the night before. When I'd finished, she put her arms around me. "I know just what it's like," she said. "My family would have acted the same way. It's really hard when your parents have been brought up in a different culture and we've been brought up as

Americans. But I also think it was mean of Greg not to understand."

I shrugged. "Someone was going to hate me whatever I did. I figured it was easier to have my family mad at me than the whole cast of the show."

"Don't worry too much," Karen said. "I'm sure they'll understand now that they've calmed down. And this will make a great story to tell your grandchildren."

"I won't have any grandchildren," I said. "After this they'll probably send me to a convent back in Mexico, or marry me off to Cousin Alfredo!"

Karen laughed, but I was serious. She hadn't seen my mother's face last night.

I went to rehearsal praying that everything would go smoothly and we could be out of there in a hurry. If I could only make it home by nine or nine-thirty, that wouldn't be too bad. But from the start I could see that the evening was doomed. The curtains wouldn't open at the end of the overture, so Drew sang the first half of his opening number invisible to the audience. Then suddenly the curtains shot open. A verse later they shot closed again.

"What's going on?" Greg yelled.

"Sorry," came Owen's voice. "Minor malfunction."

Then a backdrop got stuck and all the lights suddenly went out during Annabel's first solo. She was really mad.

"I told Greg it wasn't going to work using those geeks," she said.

It only got worse. Part of the stage started to revolve when it wasn't supposed to, making a kitchen mysteriously appear when Annabel and Drew were singing about riding in a buggy. And when we came to Justine's famous dance number, she stepped on the bottom of the gauze curtain. There was a horrible ripping sound, and the whole curtain fell, covering her in gauze.

"Get me out of here!" she screamed, fighting to get free as she stumbled around the stage. Unfortunately everyone else thought this was hysterically funny.

"Let's put this in every night. It's great," Drew said.

"Over my dead body," Justine growled. "When I get out of here, those nerds are going to wish they were far away."

I must have been the only person who wasn't laughing. I was so uptight that nothing would have made me smile. I couldn't stop thinking that my party would have started at home. The mariachi band might have shown up by now and the guests would be eating their way through all the enchiladas we'd made. And my parents would be embarrassed because I wasn't there. I missed a couple of cues in my scene with Annabel.

"Can't you get anything right?" she demanded as we came offstage. "You're making me look bad."

"That's not too hard," I muttered, but I think she heard.

Then we came to the hoedown number. My basket was now the real prop, with goodies in it. I put it over my arm and skipped out to join in the dance. As the first dancer swung me around, I suddenly realized how heavy a full basket could be. It swung out and caught on the back of Annabel's perfectly arranged curls.

"Ow!" she screamed. It took a while to get her untangled, and she made a fuss the whole time. When she was finally free she turned on me, her eyes blazing.

"Are you totally stupid or what?"

"Oh, not totally," I said, attempting to laugh it off.

But she wasn't amused. "I told Greg it was a big mistake to pick an inexperienced freshman for a big part," she said. "He seems to think you're funny, but I think he's got it wrong. It's just your natural clumsiness and stupidity that make people laugh at you."

"Annabel, cool it, please," Drew said, stepping forward before she actually attacked me.

She turned on him. "And I can't imagine what you ever saw in her. She's totally boring—no looks, no style, no personality, nothing!"

I wasn't going to take any more of this. "You think you have personality just because you're a good singer," I yelled. "But when you get offstage you're nothing but a nasty phony!"

"Why, you—"she growled, and came flying at me.

I was really only trying to defend myself, but I am kind of strong. I pushed her away from me. She flew backward and landed in the apple barrel, which didn't have any apples in it yet. She was stuck there, her legs in the air, looking pretty stupid.

"I hate you, I hate you," she screamed. "Greg, I want her out of here right now. Kick her out and bring in someone else. I'm not working with her and that's final."

"Fine," I said. "That's just fine with me. I gave up my big birthday party for this, because I didn't want to let anybody down. I can't believe I was so stupid! My family are the ones who really appreciate me!" Then I ran out of there as fast as I could.

I didn't stop running until I was outside the school grounds. Then I slowed down. It was dark and the street was almost empty except for occasional passing cars. Somehow I had to get home. I'd expected to get a ride with someone. I stood there in the darkness, not knowing what to do next. I was pretty sure that no buses ran this late, and I couldn't call my father to come get me. I'd insulted him enough without making him leave his guests.

The night wind was cold, and I realized I didn't have a jacket with me. I started to shiver, more from shock than from the cold, I think. It was just beginning to hit me what I had done. I had walked out of the play. I'd given up my one chance for stardom and success. Nobody at school would ever choose me to do anything. I was doomed to be a nobody for the rest of my life!

There were tears running down my cheeks, and I didn't even try to brush them away. Behind me I heard an engine roar to life. A sporty car shot up to me and screeched to a halt.

"What do you think you're doing?" Drew yelled.

"Going home."

"How? The last bus went hours ago."

"Then I'll walk. I don't care!" I snapped.

Drew threw back his head and laughed. "Roni, you really are something else," he said. "This is the second time I've had to come after you in a car. I think you're doing it on purpose. Get in."

"I'm not going back there," I said, "and you'll be in trouble for leaving the rehearsal."

"There is no more rehearsal," he said. "I told them if you quit I would too, and after that there didn't seem to be much point in going on."

"You did that for me?" I asked.

"Yes. Now would you please get in the car?"

I got in. Drew leaned across me to shut my door and took off at top speed.

"I don't understand," I said. "Why would you stick your neck out for me?"

"Why *wouldn't* I?" he said. "You shouldn't have to put up with that garbage from Annabel. If that had been me, I'd have pushed her into the barrel long ago. I'm just sorry the barrel wasn't full of glue . . . or paint." He glanced across and gave me his wonderful, wicked grin.

"Wait a minute," I said. "You're defending me over her?"

"Sure I am. She was totally rude to you. She's been putting you down ever since this play started."

"But I thought—" I stammered.

154

"What? That I liked Annabel? Please!"

"But I saw you," I blurted. "I saw you backstage together. You were kissing her."

"Wrong," he said.

"Well, I don't think you were giving her mouth to mouth!"

"*She* was kissing *me*," he said.

"You didn't look like you were complaining too much."

He grinned. I could see his white teeth in the darkness. "Roni, she grabbed me when we were standing backstage. She flung her arms around my neck and started kissing me. What could I do? There was a scene going on. I didn't want to interrupt the rehearsal."

"So you suffered bravely in silence," I teased. I was so happy that I felt I might burst with joy. I was sitting beside Drew in his car and it was just like old times.

"Well, a man's got to make sacrifices," he said.

"What was it like?"

"Not the greatest kiss I've ever had. Her lips were covered in cherry-flavored goop. It tasted like the stuff my dentist uses before he puts the needle in."

I started to laugh. Drew looked across at me.

"Is that why you've been acting so weird?"

I nodded. "I thought you and Annabel . . . you know."

"Well, I thought you and Chris . . . you know."

"Not anymore. I told him we could never be more than friends."

"I told Annabel we could never be more than enemies."

We laughed again. It felt so good.

"I miss you, Roni," Drew said. "Nothing was the same after we broke up. Nobody else makes me laugh the way you do."

"You mean you like being hit with flying objects?"

"I'd rather be hit with flying baskets than have to kiss cherry goop," he said, pulling up to a red light. "But only if you're the one doing the throwing."

"Anytime you want," I said.

"Although I can think of better things to do," he said.

"Like what?"

"Like this." He took my face in his hands and kissed me. "Great," he whispered. "No cherry goop."

"Oh, Drew," I said, wrapping my arms around his neck. "You don't know how I've dreamed about this happening."

"Me too," he said. "When I saw that we were in the play together, I thought it was a sign."

His eyes were shining into mine, his arms were warm around me. I never wanted this moment to end, but suddenly I remembered that I was supposed to be at a party.

"Where were we going, anyway?" Drew asked.

"Home," I said. "I've got about fifty people celebrating my birthday without me."

"Then what are we waiting for?" he said.

It was only nine o'clock when we pulled up in front of my house. Music was blaring from the patio—mariachi music with lots of trumpets. Lights were dancing in the breeze.

"Some party," he said.

"It's my fifteenth birthday," I said. "We make a big thing of that." I glanced at him, suddenly shy. "Would you like to join us?"

"Are you sure?"

I nodded. "I'd really like it, Drew. And there's plenty of good food. I should know—I've been making enchiladas nonstop for weeks."

"Great," he said. "I'm starving."

He took my hand as we walked from the car. We went around the side of the house to the patio, where most of the noise was. My mother

157

hurried past with a tray of food in her hands.

Her eyes widened. "Roni!"

"Hi, Mama. I decided the play could do without me," I said. "Drew brought me home. You remember Drew, right?"

A big smile spread across her face. "Of course," she said. "Come in. Welcome. Roni, get him something to eat. No, come with me, we must find your father. He'll be so happy you're here."

She put down her tray and grabbed my wrist, dragging me through the crowd, yelling at intervals, "Look who's here! The birthday girl's here."

A crowd of relatives closed in around me, congratulating, hugging, kissing.

I looked back at Drew, and he winked.

Chapter

13

The telephone woke me the next morning. I staggered across to answer it.

"Roni?" Boy's voice.

"Yes."

"This is your cousin Alfredo "

"Oh, Alfredo. Hi."

"I'm sorry we had to miss the party last night. We just arrived. Your mother suggested that we might do something today. I was hoping you'd show me around Phoenix."

I cursed myself for not being wider awake when I answered the phone. Then I could have pretended to be someone else and told him that Roni wasn't here. Now my brain was racing to come up with an excuse.

"Gee, I'm sorry, but I have rehearsals all day for this play tonight. Otherwise I'd have loved to."

"That's too bad," he said. "I suppose I'll just come on over to your place, then. At least I can get to know your family better."

"Wait a minute," I said. "I could ask my friends if they'd show you around Phoenix while I rehearse."

"Would you do that? That would be wonderful. I haven't had much chance to meet American girls."

"I'll call you right back," I said.

After I put the phone down, I felt like a heel. Could I really ask Ginger and Karen to spend Saturday with my cousin Alfredo? Then I decided I'd do the same for them if they were in desperate need. So I called Ginger first.

"You want me to spend the day with your cousin the blimp?"

"Please, Ginger. Like Karen said, he might have a nice personality. He sounded okay on the phone. Mama says he has a rental car. You'd just have to show him the sights and keep him away from me. I'll be in your debt forever."

"I'll remember that," she said. "In fact, I think I'll get it in writing."

"Then you'll do it?"

"I was only going to do laundry today anyway,"

she said. "I hope it's a big rental car. I don't want to be squished up against the blimp all day. You're going to ask Karen too, right? I'm not doing it alone. Anyone who wanted to get married when he was six might have weird ideas."

"Thanks, pal, buddy, wonderful friend. I'll do the same for you someday, I promise."

It was only when I'd hung up that I realized I'd forgotten to tell her about Drew.

I went to rehearsal secure in the knowledge that I was free from a pesky cousin all day—and the even better knowledge that Drew would be waiting for me.

"I thought you quit," Annabel drawled as I walked in.

"I decided the play needed at least one girl who could act," I said. "And besides, Drew wouldn't come back without me."

I went over to Drew and slipped my arm through his. It was one of the best moments of my life.

Greg appeared, looking worried. "Okay, people, we were all too stressed last night. Just forget it ever happened. Today's preview is going to be just great. No glitches, no forgotten lines, just perfect. You're going to relax and have a good time."

He came over and put an arm around my shoulders. "Look, I feel bad about making you miss your party last night," he said. "I should have understood. No hard feelings?"

I shook my head.

"Try not to let Annabel bug you," he whispered. "I know she's a pain, but she can sing."

"I know," I said. "Don't worry. I'll be fine now."

Now that I knew about Drew and me, I didn't care if Annabel turned into Freddy Kruger. Nothing she said could upset me.

Greg kept reminding us that the performance that night was only the first dress rehearsal. We were not to worry about minor details. But I was really nervous. All my family would be there, relatives I hardly knew. I just had to be good.

I was in the dressing room getting made up when Karen snuck in. "Roni, we just wanted to say break a leg," she said.

"Thanks. Oh, and thanks a million for helping out with my cousin. You don't know how much I appreciate it. How was it, pretty terrible?"

"No, not at all. In fact, I think you made a mistake, Roni. Your cousin is—"

"Cast members only," Ms. Peters said firmly. "Everyone else out, now."

Karen was driven out with all the other friends and relatives. The overture started. We took our places backstage. My knees were trembling so much that you could see my skirts shiver. I tried to remember my first line, but my mind was totally blank. What if I stepped onstage and opened my mouth and nothing came out? What if I tried to sing and I sounded like a frog?

The curtains opened, miraculously, and Drew swaggered on, singing about corn as high as an elephant's eye. He went through his scene with Annabel and they sang the buggy song with no kitchens appearing. Then it was my turn. My heart was thumping louder than the drumbeat. I stepped onstage.

Annabel said something to me and I answered. I knew the lines. They just came out. I said my first funny line and the audience laughed. After that I realized I was actually enjoying it. I loved hearing the laughter when Chris and I clowned it up. I was on cloud nine by the time we took our final bow.

After the curtain went down everybody was hugging everybody. Chris was the first to hug me. "You were great," I told him. "Don't forget me when you're a star someday."

"How could I forget you? We'll be starring in the

same Broadway show," he said, beaming.

Greg told us that we'd go over any problems on Monday, so we all made our way to meet our families and friends. I spotted my father, with Paco in his arms, just about the time Karen and Ginger grabbed me.

"You were great. Drew was great. And you were great too, Justine," they yelled as she came running up to join us. "The whole show was great," they babbled.

"You were the star," a strange voice said. A tall, dark, and incredibly gorgeous guy was standing next to my father. He held out his hand to me. "Congratulations, Roni," he said. "Finally we get to meet."

I stood there, just staring at him.

"Go on, Roni, shake hands with your cousin Alfredo," Papa urged.

I looked at Ginger and Karen.

"That's what I was trying to tell you," Karen whispered. "You were looking at the wrong person in the photo. The blimp was some friend of the family."

"I'm sorry you were not there to show me Phoenix today," Alfredo said. "But your friends were wonderful to me. We had a great time, didn't we, girls?"

"We sure did," Ginger said. They both beamed at him.

For a second I felt annoyed and jealous. That

could have been me! Then I remembered that I already had somebody special in my life.

"Your cousin suggested that all the young people go dancing tonight," Ginger said. "Good idea?"

"Just a minute," I said. "I have to check with somebody."

Drew was still in the middle of a circle of admirers. He must have sensed I was trying to get to him, because he looked in my direction and then fought his way across to me.

"Excuse me," he called, "I'm looking for a girl who can't say no!"

"Depends what the question is," I said, laughing into his eyes, "and who's asking it."

"What if it's me?" he said, laughing too as he took me in his arms.

I was conscious of my parents and relatives all hovering close by. Like Mama said, they might not understand American kidding around.

"Then the answer's later," I whispered.

Drew let go of me and I turned to see Karen, Justine, and Ginger staring at me openmouthed.

"I've got a lot to tell you guys," I said.

The next morning I stood patiently in Mama's bedroom while she helped me into the dress. She fixed my hair for me, tying it with a cascade of white ribbons. Finally I looked in the mirror.

The dress didn't look ugly anymore. The bodice fit me like a second skin. The skirt cascaded down in a shimmer of white lace. I looked pretty and special and very grown up. I kept on staring at myself, but instead of me in the mirror, I saw my mother and grandmother and generations of girls in my family all tied together by this special day.

Over my shoulder I saw that my mother was crying. "So beautiful," she murmured. "I'm so proud of you, Veronica."

And for once I wasn't annoyed that she used my full name. It seemed the right sort of name for the girl who was staring back at me from the mirror.

"I'm proud of you too, Mama," I said softly.

She gave a little confused smile. "Me? What for?"

"You're the one who had the beautiful daughter," I said lightly, but then I became serious. "And you took care of me and brought me up to know what was good and important. And you're the one who did all the hard work for today. You should be proud of yourself."

She wiped her eyes. "Oh, enough of this non-sense," she said with a laugh. "Hurry up now. Your father will be waiting."

An hour later, I walked between my parents to the front pew in church, conscious of hundreds of eyes on me. I'd never seen the church so full. Hands reached out to touch me, congratulating, admiring.

I was surprised to see Ginger's red hair and then Karen and Justine beside her. I had invited them to the reception at the parish center after the mass, of course. But I hadn't expected them to show up at the church, too. I'd told them that part would be too long and boring. It was really nice of them to want to share the whole ceremony with me. I expected them to grin or give me encouraging signs, but instead they were staring as if they didn't really believe it was me. I could hardly believe it myself.

I took my place at the very front of the church beside my family. As the priest started to pray, I glanced around. On the other side of the aisle I saw Cousin Alfredo, looking incredibly handsome in a dark suit, sitting with his mother and my other cousins. If this had been long ago, my family might have been announcing my betrothal to him today. *Not the worst thing that could happen to a girl*, I thought with a grin. *If I didn't have Drew* . . .

Then my thoughts were suddenly serious again. I was glad that this was now and not long ago. I had

167

the best of both worlds. I was free to make my own choices. I had traditions like today, but then I could go back to being myself with a whole shining future ahead of me—college, career, anything and everything was possible. I made up my mind as I sat close to my mother and father that I'd do my best to make them proud of me, whatever direction my life took.

5. GINGER'S NEW CRUSH

The ecology club is full of weirdos and nerds. So why did Ginger join? Is the real reason the fact that the the most drooled after senior in school, Scott Masters, is also a member?

6. RONI'S TWO-BOY TROUBLE

Roni had found it difficult to keep up with the high spending ways of her boyfriend Drew. But accepting $50 from the Nerds to go on a date with Chris really is going too far!

7. NO MORE BOYS

The school dance is only a few days away. But Roni's sick of boys, Karen and Ginger are mad at James and Ben, and Justine's relationship with Danny is hitting the rocks on the tennis court. Can they all be brought together in time for the dance?

8. KAREN'S LESSONS IN LOVE

Karen thinks things aren't working out with her and James. He's a really sweet guy, but she thinks there's something missing. Meanwhile, she has met someone else - - the dreamy editor of the school magazine, Damien. But is the grass always greener on the other side of the hill?